AN ILLUSTRATED TREASURY OF
SWEDISH FOLK AND FAIRY TALES

Not for individual sale to the book trade

The artwork in this book was created using methods including pencil, ink, watercolor and gouache.

English version © 2004 & 2019 Floris Books, Edinburgh
This abridged edition published in 2021 exclusively for KiwiCo

The acknowledgments on page 127 form part of the copyright agreement

All rights reserved. No part of this book may be reproduced without the prior permission of Floris Books, Edinburgh
www.florisbooks.co.uk

Printed in China through Imago

An Illustrated Treasury of
Swedish Folk and Fairy Tales

John Bauer

Floris Books

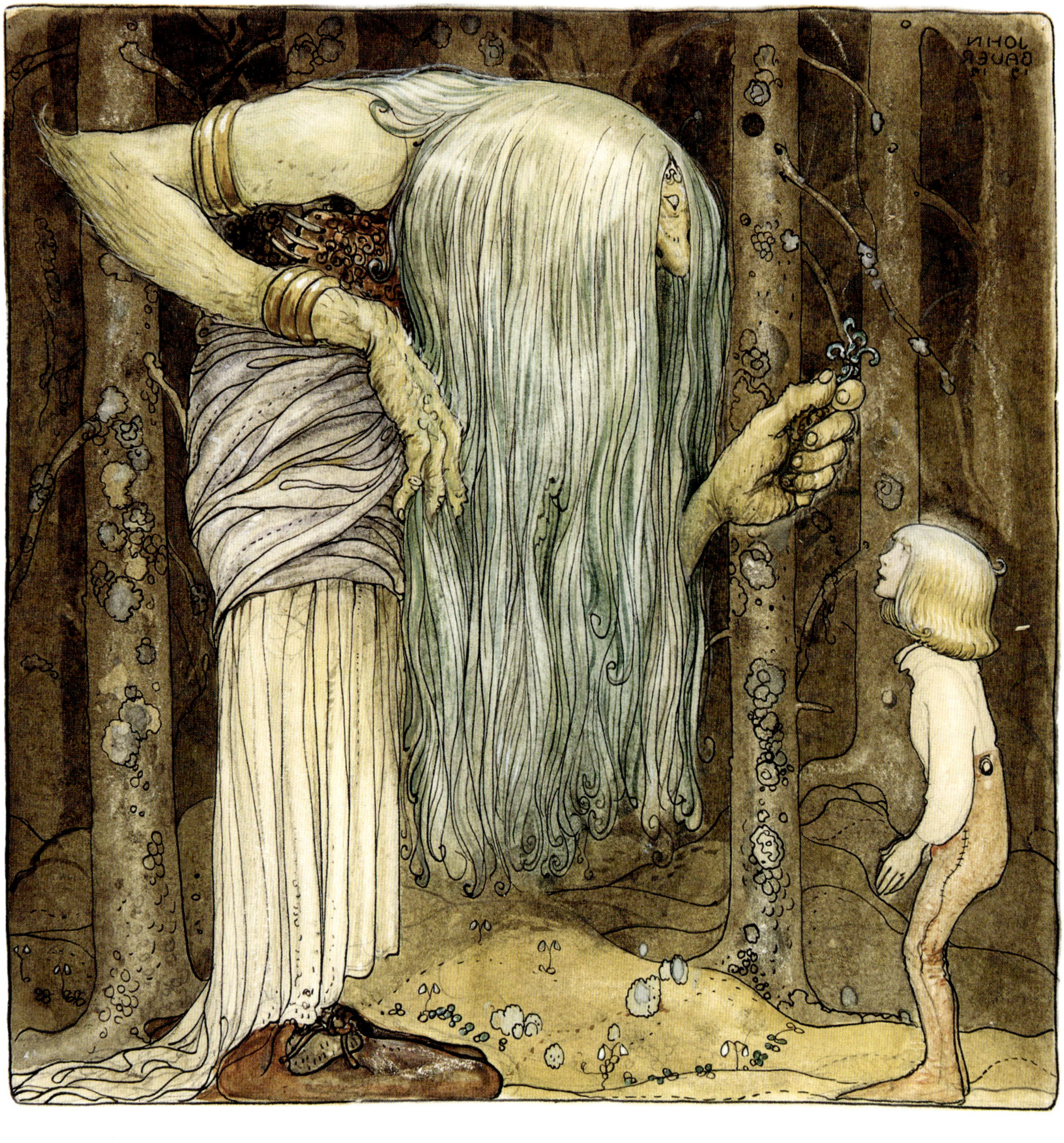
JOHN
BAUER

Contents

The Life of John Bauer ... 7

Trolls & Tomtes

The Trolls and the Youngest Tomte *Alfred Smedberg* ... 19
The Troll Ride *Anna Wahlenberg* ... 29
The Four Big Trolls and Little Peter Pastureman *Cyrus Granér* ... 37

Brave Girls & Boys

The Magician's Cape *Anna Wahlenberg* ... 55
Dag, Daga and the Flying Troll of Sky Mountain *Harald Östenson* ... 63
The Boy Who Was Never Afraid *Alfred Smedberg* ... 75

Kings & Queens

The Ring *Helena Nyblom* ... 87
Linda-Gold and the Old King *Anna Wahlenberg* ... 99
The Prince Without a Shadow *Jeanna Oterdahl* ... 105
The Queen *Anna Wahlenberg* ... 119

About the Authors ... 126
Acknowledgments ... 127

Self-portrait

The Life of John Bauer

John Bauer was one of the world's greatest illustrators of fairy tales. He was born in 1882 in the Swedish city of Jönköping, surrounded by the forests of Småland. His father came from southern Germany; his mother was Swedish. As a boy, he showed an interest in and a gift for drawing. He was uninterested in school work and spent much of his time daydreaming and doodling. Indeed, his school books were filled with caricatures — many of his teachers, to their dismay. The young Bauer also displayed a deep feeling for nature and often made long excursions on foot, alone, through the deep forests that line Lake Vättern, on the shore of which Jönköping is situated. Central to the region's myths and legends, many of which he was told by his superstitious maternal grandmother, was a belief in nature's incredible power.

When Bauer was sixteen years old he went to Stockholm, seeking to enter the Royal Academy of Arts. Despite his great talent, he was too young to be admitted. He had to wait two more years, during which time he further improved his skill as a draftsman at the Kaleb Ahltins school for painters.

At the Academy, Bauer received a traditional art education, attending lectures on classical art, perspective, anatomy and art history. He soon gained respect among both teachers and pupils. Bauer drew with serene and sure strokes, with spirited detail, and with a pronounced feeling for form. The noted Swedish painter Gustaf Cederström later compared the preciseness of Bauer's student sketches with the drawings of Dürer and Holbein, and also said, "His art is what I would call great art, in his almost miniaturized works he gives an impression of something much more powerful than many monumental artists can accomplish on acres of canvas."

A young John Bauer, circa 1890–95 (above)

John Bauer with his son Bengt (known as 'Putte') in 1917 (above right)

John Bauer at work (right)

In his spare time Bauer studied historic costumes, weapons, and buildings, and the value of this research shows itself particularly in his later fairytale illustrations. These also reflect his strong feeling for his native land — the deep forests with mossy boulders, the smiling glades, the low houses, the tarns, the mountains. Swedish nature was Bauer's favorite subject, and plants, lichens, mushrooms and mosses found in Sweden's woods are depicted in detail in his paintings.

While at the Academy, Bauer fell in love with Esther Ellqvist, a fellow student in the women's department. A talented artist in her own right, Ellqvist also modeled for

Rottrollen (The Root Trolls)

Bauer throughout their relationship. He painted her for the first time in 1904, in *Sagoprinsessan* (*The Fairy Princess*). The couple married in 1906, and settled down in Villa Björkudden on the shore of Lake Bunn in 1914. Their son Bengt (nicknamed Putte) was born in 1915, and the painting *Rottrollen* (*The Root Trolls*) features him asleep in a forest among troll-shaped roots.

Bauer's career as a painter of fairy tales began while he was still a student, when he was commissioned to illustrate Anna Wahlenberg's book *Länge, länge sedan* (*Long, Long Ago*). Three years later he made his real breakthrough when the annual *Julstämning* (*Christmas Spirit*), under the aegis of Cyrus Granér, began publishing the collection *Bland tomtar och troll* (*Among Tomtes and Trolls*), which came out once a year. Eight of the first ten editions were illustrated entirely by Bauer, and his clumsy, strangely natural-looking troll figures were soon beloved by every Swede. He illustrated the work of almost every well-known Swedish storyteller, the best of whom are represented in this collection. Generations of Scandinavian children have been brought up among his pictures, both in their books and on their walls.

Bauer's working methods were painstaking. His first illustrations for stories began as thumbnail sketches placed side by side in sequence, almost like a comic book. Gradually he would develop each sketch, increasing the size and reworking details, such as the shape of a branch, until finally he was ready to paint.

In early volumes of *Among Tomtes and Trolls*, limited printing technology meant that Bauer's paintings could only be reproduced in black and yellow. By 1912 blue was added to this color palette, so the reproductions could resemble Bauer's original artworks more closely. Nevertheless, Bauer made sparing use of color, feeling that muted tones better suited the mysterious woodland settings of his illustrations and stimulated readers' imaginations. In a 1953 interview, Bauer's friend Ove Eklund said that Bauer believed the creatures he drew actually existed.

Yet Bauer wished to pursue other artistic goals too. In 1915 he left *Among Trolls and Tomtes* to take his art in a different direction. After the onset of the First World War, he felt unable to imagine the world as a fairy tale any longer. Also, he had long felt a strong urge towards other kinds of expression, such as oil painting, frescos and set design for theatre, but was never able to fulfil this ambition.

In 1918, he, Esther and Bengt, only three years old, were on their way to their new home in Stockholm. Bauer had booked passage by boat because of a recent train accident that had been in the news. The Bauers were among the passengers on the steamer *Per Brahe* which, on a dark November night, sank in Lake Vättern. All on board were drowned.

John Bauer was only 36 years old, and the world had lost one of its most exciting, creative visionaries.

From *The Flower of Happiness on Sunnymount Crest* by Alfred Smedberg

From *The Boy and the Tomte's Hat* by Vilhälm Nordin

TROLLS & TOMTES

All this happened long ago, when there were trolls in the dark mountains and the big dusky forests...

From *The Giant Who Slept for Ten Thousand Years* by Einar Rosenborg

From *The Boy and the Tomte's Hat* by Vilhälm Nordin

From *The Giant Who Slept for Ten Thousand Years* by Einar Rosenborg

From a Christmas book

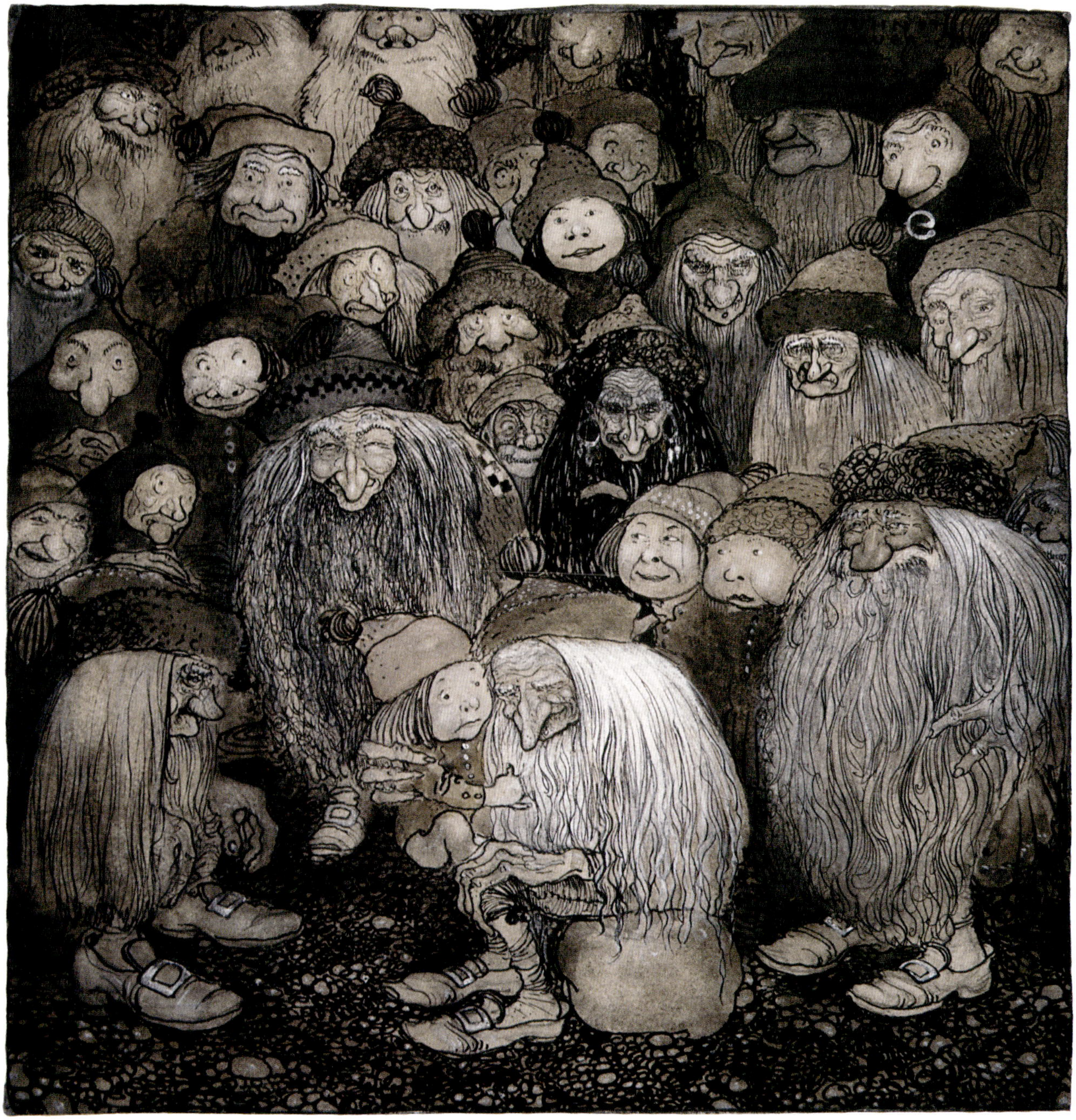

The Trolls and the Youngest Tomte

Alfred Smedberg

In a storehouse on a small farm at the edge of a wood lived three tomtes: Tjarfa, Torgus, and Tjovik. They were part of an old tomte family that had lived on the farm for more than nine hundred years. The farm had changed owners many times. Old people had gone away and new ones had come, but the tomte family had faithfully remained, and the honor of being the tomte who looked after the farm passed from father to son.

The little storehouse was situated prettily between hilly pastureland and a dense, dark forest. In the forest was steep, craggy Foxhall Mountain. Two trolls lived there: Jompa and Skimpa, the troll king of the mountain and his wife. They had lived there long before people moved in alongside them, and were four thousand years old.

The tomtes and the trolls had always been bitter enemies. The trolls were large, strong, evil, and stupid; the tomtes were as small as dolls, but kind and very intelligent. The trolls wanted to hurt the people on the farm, which is why the tomtes hated them. They were always fighting. Sometimes the tomtes won, sometimes the trolls. It could not be otherwise, since it was a battle between strength and intelligence.

Now it was Christmas Eve, and a feast was being held in the storehouse, where Grandfather tomte, Tjarfa Jorikson, lived between a couple of flour barrels. It was the old one's five-hundredth birthday, and his birthday and Christmas were to be celebrated together this year. Grandfather Tjarfa was brisk and active despite his age, but had recently retired and handed down his authority to Torgus Tjarfson, who was three hundred years old and in the prime of life. The youngest tomte, Tjovik Torgusson, was a boy of only one hundred years. He did not even have a tomte beard yet, and he scarcely reached his father's shoulder.

All the tomtes in the region had been invited to the party, and they were all in high spirits. The storehouse was well stocked with apples, loaves of wort bread, ham, and sausage, all spread out on a small table that was really an upturned sugar-box. The farm people knew that the tomtes were careful, never wasting so much as a spoonful of flour.

"Now, Grandfather, tell us stories about Skimpa and Jompa," said Tjovik, climbing up into the old tomte's lap and stroking his long white beard.

"Well, my grandson," said the old tomte happily, "sit still and you shall hear about how it used to be."

༈

All the tomtes made themselves comfortable. Some lay on the floor, hands under chins; others sat and dangled their legs from anchovy-tin chairs.

Old Tjarfa began: "I shall tell how it was eight hundred years ago, when my grandfather Tarja Torgusson was in his prime, on Foxhall Mountain. People had decided to build a church on the plain, but the trolls were angry about it, so every night they tore down what had been built the day before."

"But the church was built, wasn't it?" said little Tjovik.

"It was indeed, and it was Grandfather Tarja who helped build it. He filled a bag with ashes and climbed a tree growing on the mountain. When the trolls came out of the mountain at night to throw boulders at the church, he threw ashes in their eyes."

"And the trolls could not see the church!" cried the delighted tomtes.

"They could not. There was an outcry from the trolls, who threw their boulders but never hit the mark."

"Poor Jompa," giggled the boy tomte.

"And so the church was finished," continued old Tjarfa. "The bishop blessed it, and after that the trolls could not damage it. But they were all the wilder in the forest. At that time there were wolves and bears, and the trolls encouraged them to attack farm animals. Grandfather always had to fly back and forth like a shuttlecock to help the farm folk."

"Did the trolls ever catch him?" asked Tjovik.

"Oh yes. Many times they took him into the mountain, but he always tricked them and escaped. Sometimes he came out sooty and scratched, but other times he brought out more gold than he could carry."

"Do the trolls have gold in the mountain?" asked Tjovik, surprised.

The other tomtes laughed until their beards shook. "It's clear you are just a child, little Tjovik," they said, "or else you would know that Foxhall Mountain is full of gold and jewels."

"Really?" exclaimed the boy tomte. "Then shouldn't we go and get some of the treasure? The poor people around here need a few luxuries to brighten their lives."

"No, my little boy," said his father crossly. "Troll gold is never a blessing; it only leads to pride, laziness, greed, strife, fighting, and hatred. My grandfather taught me this early, and for that reason my father and I and all the tomtes here have left the mountain gold untouched."

"It must be hard to find anyway," mused Tjovik.

"Well, tonight it would be easy," replied the old grandfather. "On Christmas Eve the trolls bring out all their treasure to count it, and they are so eager and excited that they don't notice a thing around them."

"But how would someone get into the mountain?" asked Tjovik.

"On Christmas Eve the mountain doors swing open by themselves," was the reply. "But woe to anyone who is still there when the churchbells ring for matins. Then the trolls both see and hear, and you are trapped."

"Did your father ever have trouble with them, Grandfather?"

"Jovik Tarjason, I should say so! Once he was within a hairsbreadth of losing his life. That time he rode an ox out of the mountain."

"What happened, dear Grandfather? Tell us, tell us."

"Well, you see, Skimpa had stolen the ox from the farm. My father was furious, so he crept into the mountain. It was easy, for the troll woman had forgotten to shut the door. Jompa was standing there with an axe raised over the head of the ox, ready to kill it. Well, Father was bold. He climbed up the ox's tail and pricked its back with a pin. The ox jumped, knocked over both Skimpa and Jompa, and they fell to the floor with their feet in the air. Then the ox tore out of the mountain door with Father on its back."

The tomtes laughed so hard that two of them fell off the anchovy tin.

"And you, Grandfather. Have you ever been inside the mountain?" asked Tjovik.

"Many times, but I have never taken anything from the trolls except what they had stolen from our farm people. Once I barely escaped with my life. I lost my red tasseled cap and my wooden shoes, and had to go up the chimney to get away because the doors were locked. I came home sooty as a sweep."

"My brother had the same bad luck a few years ago," said another tomte.

"What happened to him?" Tjovik asked.

"He was trying to find a young shepherdess whom the trolls had carried away, and he was in the mountain when the cock crowed and all the doors shut with a bang. There was nothing for him to do but throw himself into the mountain spring and go underground with the stream. The brook that flows through the farm has its source in the mountain, you know. The poor man was soaked to the skin when he came home."

The young tomte listened to all this with the greatest interest. He would very much have liked to snatch a bracelet or a golden chain from the trolls to give to Anna Lisa, the farmer's oldest daughter, who was soon to be married. She was good to everyone, and Tjovik wished her the very best of fortune.

The tomtes sat and listened to old Tjarfa for a long time, until at last they all became sleepy and trooped off home. Grandfather fell asleep on an old mitten in a corner of the storeroom, and Torgus and Tjovik lay down on a mat between a couple of sugar boxes.

But the young tomte could not go to sleep. He was wondering how he could fetch Anna Lisa a treasure from the mountain, just one. Surely there could be no harm in that. Surely it was only when you took too much gold that you became wicked. At last he sat up, put his cap on his head and his wooden shoes on his feet, picked up his little stick, and set out for the forest.

The night was dark and silent. Not a star winked from heaven and not a gleam of light shone from any of the cottage windows. Everything dreamed in a deep, quiet, midnight sleep, and only the drawn-out howl of a fox could now and then be heard from the forest. The tomte boy trotted along quickly. He was not afraid of the dark and did not care about the fox. When you have legs only three inches long, you cannot go very fast, and the little tomte took five steps for every one a human would have taken. Yet he did make progress, and in an hour he was at the foot of Foxhall Mountain.

My, how craggy and steep and high it rose! From deep inside there came a tinkling, clanking sound, as if someone were rattling and jingling gold and silver coins.

"You just wait," said Tjovik, and began to climb the mountain.

It was slow going, but he managed it somehow. Sometimes he slipped, but then he took fresh hold and climbed higher and higher. Breathless and hot and sweaty, he climbed from crag to crag, rock to rock, and swung himself up one ledge after another until he was halfway up the mountainside.

An owl hooted from a nearby grove, but Tjovik would not let himself be scared. He would climb until he found an opening. At last he saw a faint light through a small crack in the rocks. He poked his little stick into the opening and twisted it. The door must have been well greased, for it opened slowly and soundlessly on its hinges.

Now the little tomte entered a vast hall of rugged black stone with rusty weapons hanging on the walls. He saw the bones of big cattle here and there on the floor, and it was dismal and gloomy. He walked on.

He came to a second door, which seemed to be made of copper. It opened as easily as the first, and Tjovik stepped into another hall. Silver coins were heaped against the walls, but not a creature was in sight. *Surely there is enough money here to buy a watch for the good farmer,* he thought. *But wait! What is that tinkling and jingling on the other side of that silver door? I wonder what they are doing in there.*

He padded silently to the silver door, opened it, and what did he see? An open chest in the middle of the floor and two terrible trolls sitting beside it, jingling and rattling gold rings, bracelets, pearls, and precious stones. They were so busy counting the treasure in their chest that they neither saw nor heard Tjovik enter.

On the far side of the hall was a well where water rushed up from the rock and earth below. An old cracked wooden shoe was in the well, tied to the wall with a string to keep it from being washed away.

Skimpa must have put that wooden shoe in the well to make the wood swell, thought Tjovik. *I could always sail away from here in that if the doors are closed.*

He approached the chest quietly and carefully, but to him it was so high he could not reach the top. He stretched and stretched on tiptoe, as far as he could, and then what do you think happened?

Jompa and Skimpa sneezed, both at the same time. My goodness, how it echoed through the mountain! The sneezes lifted the little tomte into the air like a feather, and he landed headfirst right in the middle of all the gold in the chest. *It's all over now,* thought Tjovik, holding tightly to his stick to defend himself from the trolls.

But those stupid trolls had not seen him! They just kept counting and counting. Tjovik looked around at all the gold and treasure. He picked out a chain just long enough to hang around someone's neck, and tried to climb to the edge of the chest and jump to the floor.

That was when all the churchbells down below began to chime, calling the congregations to morning prayers. Both trolls jumped up and stuck their fingers in their ears. Then they closed and locked the mountain doors, and slammed down the lid of the chest on the gold, and on the little tomte boy.

Poor Tjovik sat there like a mouse in a trap, but he was not one to lose courage easily. *If only I can trick the trolls into opening the chest again, I can get away,* he thought. He put his mouth to the keyhole and began to squeak like a mouse.

"There's a rat in there!" cried the troll woman.

"Let it stay till next Christmas, for all I care," said the old man.

"But it will gnaw a hole through the chest," the woman replied.

"You might be right," her husband admitted.

And so they opened the chest again and saw the little tomte sitting near the edge.

"My, what a funny-looking little rat," said the troll, and laughed until his belly shook. "What kind of a snippet are you?"

"I am Tjovik Torgusson, a tomte from the farm," Tjovik answered fearlessly.

"Ha, ha, ha! Hi, hi, hi! Ho, ho, ho!" laughed the troll, and took Tjovik between his thumb and forefinger. "He will make a fine dessert after the Christmas ham. Have you a frying pan ready, Mother?"

"You can't fry me before I've washed the dirt off my fingers," said Tjovik.

"Hold your tongue," warned the troll. "You'll be washed all right, and you can be sure of that." And he put the boy on the brim of the well and poured water all over him.

"I'm still dirty!" Tjovik cried. "You had better get a scrubbing brush and some soap."

"You're a fussy little man," grumbled the troll, but he loosened his grip and went to fetch a scrubbing brush.

Instantly, the tomte jumped into the wooden shoe, opened his knife, and cut off the string that anchored the shoe to the wall. Heigh-ho! Right away the wooden shoe began to float on the stream that flowed down the mountain well. Jompa and Skimpa howled loud enough to break your eardrums, but the little tomte just waved his pointed red cap and called "Hurrah!"

The rapids carried him and the wooden shoe through an underground channel and out again into the brook that ran by the farm. There, Tjovik jumped ashore and made his way home. But he had no treasure: he had dropped the golden chain when the troll dashed water over him.

It was a close thing whether Tjovik would get a good thrashing from both his father and grandfather for his foolish adventure, but he escaped punishment because he had never done anything wrong before. He had to promise never again to look for treasure, except for that which can be earned through honest work. And this is a promise he has never broken.

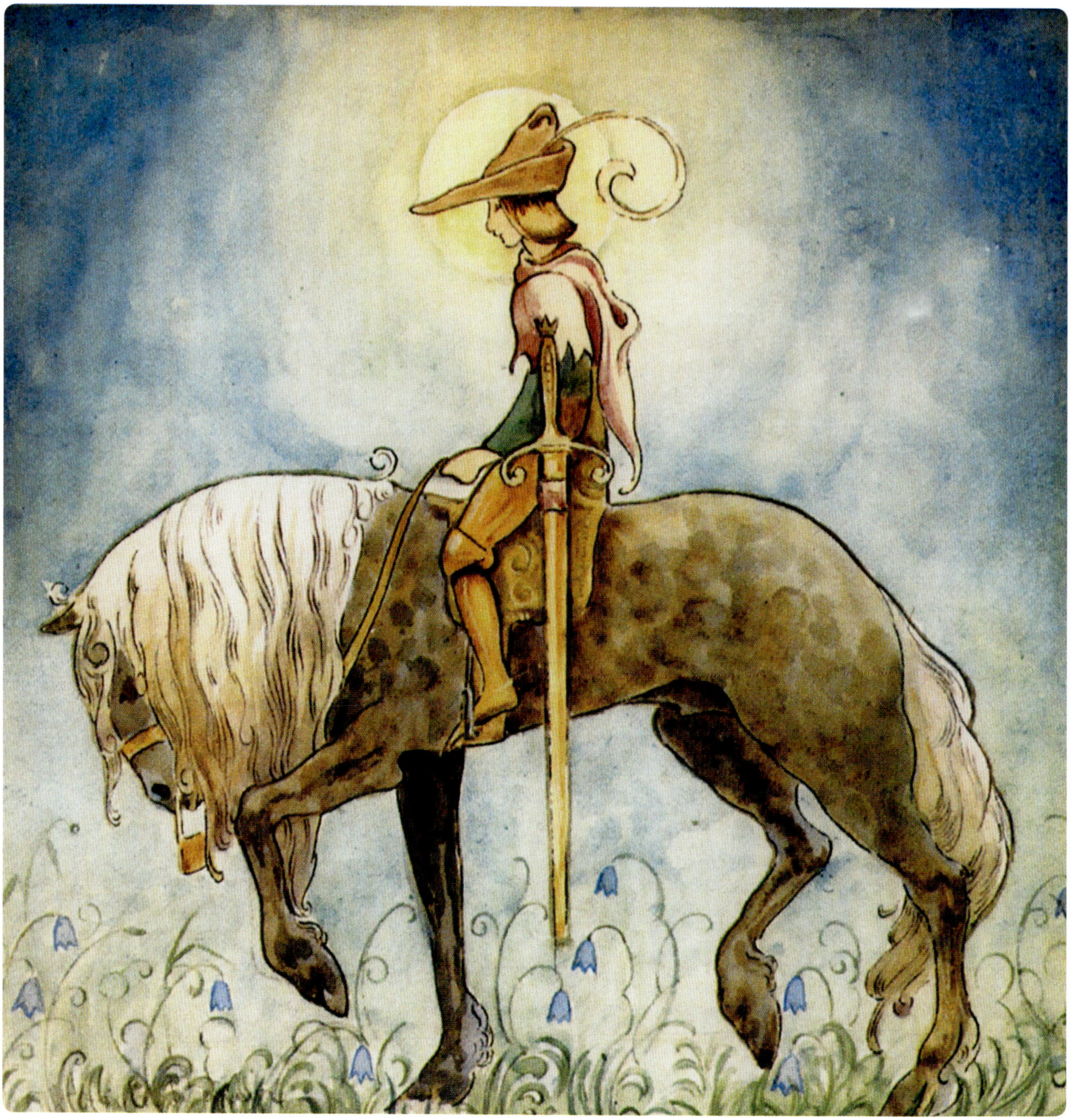

The Troll Ride

Anna Wahlenberg

Peder Lars rode along the highway, his heart singing. He was bound for the city to buy a new jacket, because that evening he was going a-courting and wanted to look his best. He felt rather sure that the rich and proud Lisa would not turn him down: although Peder Lars was the poorest of all her admirers, she always looked at him kindly, and she had agreed that he and his father might come to visit her at six o'clock.

Peder Lars rode across fields and into a long, deep forest, then he emerged onto a green meadow. Suddenly he saw something moving in a ditch. He drew nearer and realized it was a strange-looking woman, crawling along.

She lifted her head and stared at him. He had never before seen anything as evil-looking as her face. Her small peppercorn eyes were almost hidden in matted hair. Her nose looked like a carrot, and her lips were dry as bread crust.

"Will you do me a good turn?" she asked. "I shall reward you for your trouble."

"What is it?" asked Peder Lars.

The woman said that she had hurt her leg wandering in the forest and had limped this far because in the next wood, near a path that climbed a hill, there grew seven pine trees. A little resin from each of these pines rubbed into her wound would make the pain go away immediately. But before she got very far she had collapsed and so was lying here helpless in the ditch. She badly needed someone to collect resin from the wood for her. She would see that he was well rewarded for his trouble. Already, five people had accepted a gold coin for saying they would help, but they had probably taken the money and found another road home, because she had not seen any of them again.

Peder Lars stepped back. "How do you come to have so many gold coins? Who are you?"

The woman moaned and rubbed her leg. "Oh, how it hurts! And my mother is walking in the forest looking for me and calling me. Listen, can you hear?"

"No, I don't hear anything," said Peder Lars. Suddenly the woman grabbed the mane of his horse, pulled herself up, and put her hand like a trumpet to his ear. Now he heard someone singing deep in the forest:

>*Where are you, daughter, sweet and fair?*
>*I'm looking for you everywhere.*

Peder Lars could not help laughing, because he did not think that 'sweet and fair' really suited the woman by his side.

The woman sank back down into the ditch, but she peered over the edge, and her small peppercorn eyes shot fiery glances.

"You laugh, like all the rest, and hate me!" she hissed. "But I will give you money, as much money as you want, if only you will get me that pine resin." She rattled the gold coins in her fist.

Peder Lars stared at her. Then he knocked her hand so that all the gold coins fell into the ditch.

"No, thank you," he said. "You are a troll, and I don't want to have anything to do with a troll." And he cracked his whip and continued his journey.

He rode into the city, bought himself a smart jacket, and turned homewards again. Yet when he came to the hill that the woman had mentioned, he could not help looking around for the seven pine trees. There they stood in a row, murmuring softly. At that moment he heard someone singing far, far away:

>*Where are you, daughter, sweet and fair?*
>*I'm looking for you everywhere.*

He quickly checked the pine trunks for resin, but it was hard to find any now that the afternoon light was fading.

No, I must hurry, he thought, *or I'll reach Lisa late, and that might cost me dearly.* And so he rode on.

He had gone only a little farther when his horse stopped by itself and pricked up its ears, listening. Once again he heard the song:

Where are you, daughter, sweet and fair?
I'm looking for you everywhere.

If only I had time to gather some of that resin, he thought, and turned around. But after a minute he changed his mind. "It's madness," he said to himself. "What do I care about an ugly old troll woman?" And so he turned homewards again.

It did not take long before the horse stopped again and once more he heard the song:

Where are you, daughter, sweet and fair?
I'm looking for you everywhere.

I can't bear it, thought Peder Lars. *If I don't get the resin, I'm afraid I will never stop hearing that song!* And so he galloped back to the pine trees.

He examined the trunks and branches, and at last he gathered resin from each of the seven trees. By now it was almost dark, so he galloped along the road. He came to the ditch and saw the troll woman still sitting there.

"Here you are, old hag," he shouted, throwing the resin into her lap. "And I hope I never see you again, for you have probably cost me my sweetheart's hand in marriage."

He spurred his horse on without waiting to hear whether or not the woman would thank him. He was angry and anxious, sure that he would be too late. What would Lisa's father say? Peder Lars knew he was not happy about the prospect of having a pauper for a son-in-law. Peder's lateness would give him an excuse to refuse his daughter's hand. And Lisa herself? Her pride might be hurt.

Suddenly he heard hooves ahead, and from round a bend in the road his brother approached him on horseback. He looked a sight, and his horse was all in a lather.

"You'll be late, you'll be late!" his brother called. And as the two of them galloped on together, he told Peder Lars that their old father had been waiting by Lisa's farm-gate for Peder Lars to come when suddenly the rich miller Jonas, who owned half the village, had pulled up in his carriage. He too was going to ask for the beautiful Lisa's hand. If Peder Lars was turned down, he said, then he was ready to take his place. And so there Jonas sat now, waiting. It was now a quarter to six and they had several miles to go.

"Goodbye," Peder Lars called, urging his horse to the utmost and streaking along the forest path at breakneck speed. It was so dark that he could hardly see the road before him. Branches tore at his handsome new jacket and scratched his forehead until it bled, but he paid no attention. All Peder Lars could think was that the beautiful Lisa might give her hand to the rich miller Jonas to punish him for being late. *That is what I get for having anything to do with trolls,* he thought.

Soon his horse began to pant and stumble and trip, and Peder Lars was afraid it might collapse under him. The horse went slower and slower, no matter how he urged it forward.

Then he felt the reins go taut in his hands. The horse lifted its head and its hooves began to fly over the ground, so fast that Peder Lars' cape billowed behind.

He felt sure that someone was sitting behind him on the horse's back. He turned around, and although no one was there, he imagined he saw what looked like a gray bundle slip down over the horse's rump.

The ride became wilder and wilder, as the horse no longer followed the road but turned in among bushes and undergrowth. It jumped hillocks and streams, and Peder Lars no longer felt in control of the reins. Every time he cast a look behind, he dimly glimpsed a gray bundle sliding farther back on the horse. And every time he looked ahead, he felt more and more sure that someone was sitting behind him.

Peder Lars' cape was flying straight up over his head, stretched as trim as a sail. The horse flew like a bird and its hooves barely touched ground. They reached the road again and met his old father, who shook his head sadly.

"You will never get there. You have only a minute left."

"We'll see," Peder Lars called, and disappeared so fast that the old man did not even see him go.

At the farmer's house, everyone was waiting. Beautiful Lisa, her arm leaning on the windowsill, was listening for the beat of hooves, while her father and Jonas the miller rubbed their hands contentedly.

"Now," said her father, looking at the clock on the wall, "there is only half a minute to go. If he were going to come on time, we would have heard his horse on the bridge by now. Lisa, you may as well give the miller your hand right away, for you will never be satisfied with a suitor who keeps you waiting."

"I will wait until six o'clock," Lisa said, her heart beating fast. Though her father was right, and she was so proud that she would rather make herself unhappy for the rest of her life than be kept waiting a single second by a suitor, it would be desperately hard to lose Peder Lars.

The clock began to chime.

"Too late!" cried the miller.

Then they heard the strong beat of hooves on the bridge, and Lisa's eyes shone with joy. "Listen, he is coming!" she exclaimed.

"Too late," said her father.

But just as the clock was ready to chime for the sixth time, the door was flung open and there stood Peder Lars, dripping wet, his hair tousled, and his new jacket dusty and torn, yet he looked jaunty and dashing all the same. Lisa ran to him and put her hand in his, so firmly and confidently that Peder Lars knew she was giving it to him for life.

The miller and the farmer could only gape. They could not understand how Peder Lars had managed to arrive on time, and no one else understood either.

But this was not the last time people would marvel at Peder Lars. From then on, regardless of how late he set out on any journey, he would always arrive on time. Whether he rode on horseback or in a carriage, he was calm and assured. And he could well afford to be, for he always felt he had someone with him, someone who made sure that all his adventures always finished well. But who this was he never could discover, no matter how many times he turned his head and thought he glimpsed a gray bundle slip down the rump of his horse or off the edge of his carriage. Yet inside himself Peder Lars knew who it was that sat behind him.

He had not asked any reward for the favor he had done for the troll in the ditch, but a reward he certainly did receive.

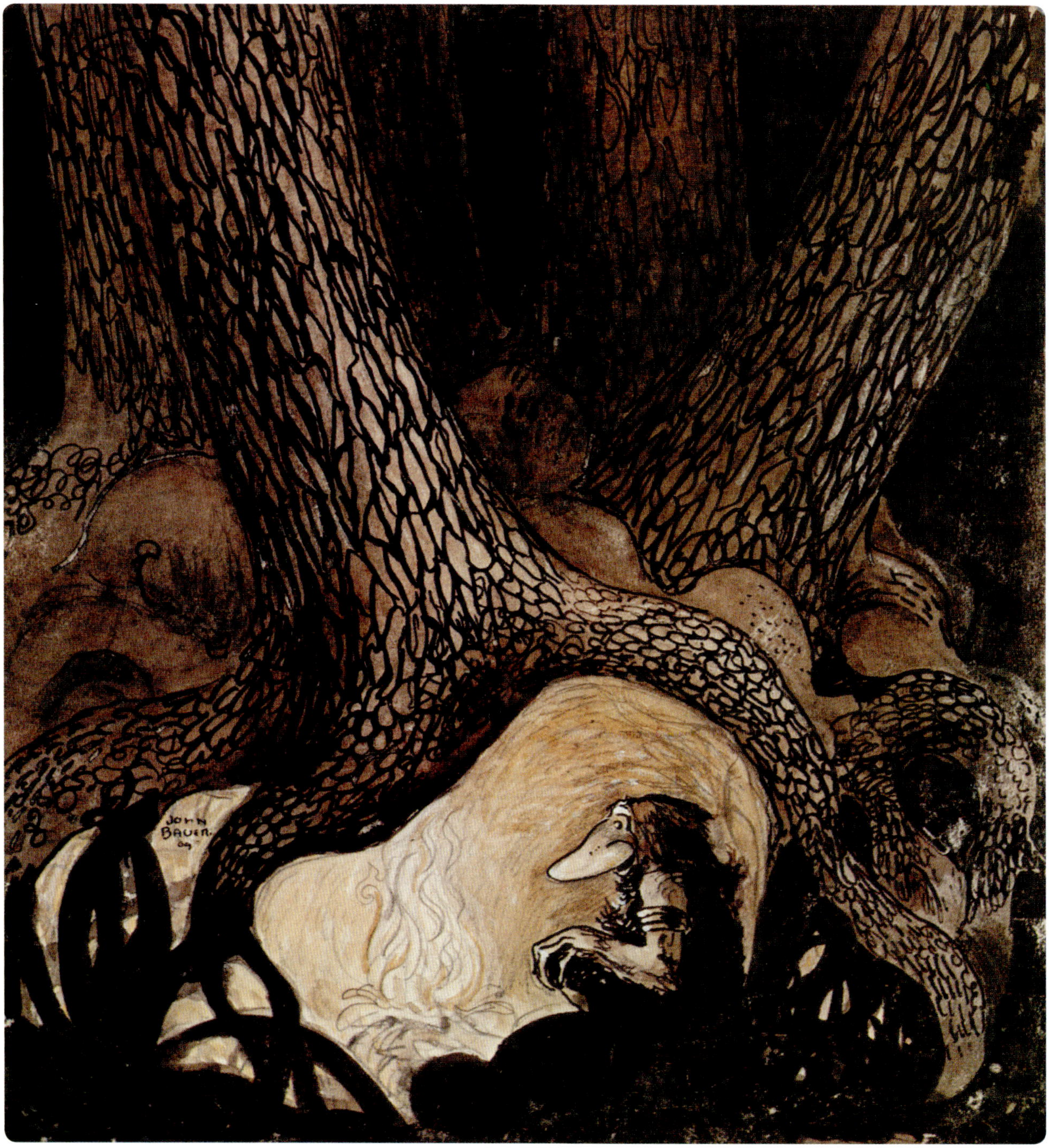
JOHN
BAUER
09

The Four Big Trolls and Little Peter Pastureman

Cyrus Granér

All this happened long, long ago, when there were trolls in the dark mountains and the big dusky forests. Each cave on a craggy mountainside, each hollow under the snakelike roots of giant trees, had its own troll living there. Some trolls lived alone; others had a wife and child. There were big trolls and little trolls, and naturally the big trolls thought they were superior to the little trolls.

The four biggest trolls counted themselves most important of all: Bull-Bull-Bulsery-Bull, who lived in the north; Drull-Drull-Drulsery-Drull, who had settled in the east; Klampe-Lampe from the south; and Trampe-Rampe, who liked wandering but said his home was in the west.

Many long miles separated the trolls from each other, but it didn't seem far to them. Twelve miles to a step was nothing for a big troll, and in half a day any of them could visit the others. They did not do this often, however, because they did not get along very well. Each wanted to be the most important big troll and looked down upon the others.

Bull-Bull-Bulsery-Bull lived on Bunner Mountain, and he was as cosy there as a troll could wish. Just in front of his mountain was a lake big enough for Bull to use as both a bathing pool and a fishpond. Bull was very proud of his lake, for he had made it himself. One day he had thrown a strong troll rope around an acre of land, harnessed up his two troll oxen, and pulled the land away. Then he arranged for old Whitebeard, master of Snowfall Mountain, to supply him with water all the year round. And old Whitebeard filled his lake with water clear as crystal and cool as the morning wind on High Mountain.

Drull lived well too in the big, deep chambers of his den on Steep Mountain, splendid in a thousand ways. On top of his den he had placed a large boulder from which he could stand and look out over the still, dreamlike, mighty forests.

Klampe-Lampe had dug himself a large hole under seven immense spruce trees. It was warm and pleasant there, and most of the time Klampe-Lampe stayed at home guarding the thousand-year-old fire on his hearth.

Trampe-Rampe was seldom so still. He ranged far and wide over the mountains and would go racing by when you least expected to see him. You would hear his storm song, then the next moment he was sweeping by with a hi and a ho.

✥

The little trolls were so numerous it was quite impossible to keep track of them. And yet we must not forget to mention little Peter Pastureman.

Peter Pastureman was small even next to a little troll, and he hardly reached the waist of a big one, but he was a real thunderclap of a boy. He worked for the four biggest trolls: he drove Bull's oxen, herded Drull's goats, caught Klampe-Lampe's unruly rams, and rode Trampe-Rampe's fast horses. None of this was easy to do, yet Peter Pastureman never wanted to be more than a farmhand. He had a birchbark horn and a reed whistle to blow on, and they resounded over bog and forest, and he was cheerful and merry, rain or shine.

We must also remember an old troll witch who was wiser than anyone under the stars. Whenever the trolls wanted to do anything important and were not sure how to go about it, they always asked her advice. Her name was Uggle-Guggle, and she lived in an old cottage in the densest part of the wild forest.

Now, as we said, the big trolls were not friends, and if any one of them could play a trick on another, he was delighted. He would go about chuckling to himself, thinking it wonderful to be so shrewd and cunning, until the other had found a way to trick him in turn, whereupon his joy turned to anger and he hissed like nineteen north winds.

Peace, more or less, had reigned for a while among the four big trolls when something happened to make them even worse enemies than ever.

One day the good old troll king in Seven Mile Mountain, king of all the world's trolls and tomtes, entered the dark gorge in Black Mountain, and its door closed behind him forever. Never again would they be able to look at him, never touch his hand, never hear wise and beautiful words from his lips. He had ruled for three thousand years and been revered as no troll king ever was before. But now the trolls had to find a new king.

There were many who wanted to be his successor. It would be finer than the sun and moon to be king of all the big and little trolls and tomtes and sprites; to live in Seven Mile Mountain, which had seven hundred magnificent halls and chambers; to own all those oxen with gilded horns, goats with silver hair, horses with golden manes, and so many other wonderful things. So now the four big trolls dreamt day and night about becoming king.

Bull believed he was destined to be king. Drull knew none could deserve the honor more than he. Klampe-Lampe let it be known that he would be the most logical choice even if you scoured the troll world five hundred times. Trampe-Rampe was willing to wager his big nose that, as king, he could surpass all before him.

These days, when they met, the four biggest trolls would not even look at one another. Each was so furious with the rest he would have liked to grind them to powder, for each imagined that, but for the other three, he would naturally become the new king. The longer the troll council debated whom to choose, the angrier the four became and the harder they considered how to win the throne in Seven Mile Mountain.

✢ ✥ ✢

The big day arrived, and the troll council still had not come to a decision. They all went home and thought for seven more days, but it didn't help. They thought about it for seven days longer and still could not decide. So they decided they would visit Uggle-Guggle, the troll witch who was wiser than anyone under the stars, and ask her advice.

When Bull learned of this plan, he thought it would be sensible to make sure he was in the old woman's good graces, so he decided to pay her a call. With his walking stick in hand, he took the road that led to the densest part of the wild forest. He walked along carefully, keeping an eye open, for naturally he did not want anyone to know what he was doing. At last he arrived at the cottage and knocked on the door.

The old witch received him. "A distinguished visitor," she said.

"Yes," said Bull. "I was passing through the neighborhood and wanted to see how you were getting on all on your own here."

They began to talk and finally Bull brought up the subject of being king. "Help me in this," he said, "you who are wiser than anyone under the stars, and I shall give you the best golden cow in Seven Mile Mountain, as sure as my name is Bull."

At that moment there came a heavy knock on the door.

"Oh, dear, Mother Uggle-Guggle," cried Bull, "you must hide me, for no one must know I have been here."

The old woman pushed him up to the attic, and then went to open the door.

It was Drull. He had had exactly the same idea as Bull.

"A distinguished visitor," said the witch.

"Yes," said Drull. "I was just passing by and thought it would be nice to see if you were well, old Mother."

They talked of this and that, and at last Drull brought up what was on his mind. "Help me to Seven Mile Mountain," he said, "and you shall receive the best golden cow there is, as sure as my name is Drull."

But matters turned out no better for Drull than for Bull. Before the witch had time to answer, a loud clap sounded on the door. Someone else wanted to come in.

Drull, frightened at being discovered, begged the witch to hide him. The old woman lifted the cellar door and down he crept. Then she went to open the cottage door.

This time it was Klampe-Lampe who had also had the idea of talking to Uggle-Guggle, and was delighted with himself for being so cunning.

"A distinguished visitor," said the witch.

"Yes," said Klampe-Lampe. "The weather was so fine that I thought I would take a little stroll around the countryside, and when I passed I thought it would be nice to call and see how you were these days, dear Mother."

Then he talked for a while about different things, of this and that, and at last he offered, "If you will help me to the throne in Seven Mile Mountain, I shall give you its biggest and most magnificent cow to keep forever."

But Klampe-Lampe learned no more than Bull or Drull about what the witch thought of his offer, for once again the door shook with a heavy knock.

"I must hide," cried Klampe-Lampe. "You realize what it would mean if anyone saw me here!"

The old witch pushed him into her large empty oven and shut the door with a mighty bang.

"I wonder if perhaps it isn't Trampe-Rampe thundering out there," mumbled Uggle-Guggle to herself. "Wouldn't it be strange if he too had decided to look in on me just now?"

It *was* Trampe-Rampe.

"A distinguished visitor," said the witch.

"Yes," said Trampe-Rampe. "I have been out on a long walk and was beginning to feel tired and wanted a rest a while before I set off again. But since I am here, I will mention a certain matter which is very important, and get your advice — you who are wiser than anyone under the stars."

So Bulsery-Bull, Drulsery-Drull, and Klampe-Lampe had to lie there and listen to Trampe-Rampe fawning over the old crone and promising her gold and a life of splendour if only she would put in a good word for him.

How strange! He did not receive his advice either, for just then came a fresh banging at the door. Eager voices were heard outside. Messengers from the troll council had come to consult the witch. By the time they entered, Trampe-Rampe had disappeared; Uggle-Guggle had hidden him in a shed out the back, and there he would wait until the coast was clear.

The messengers explained to the witch why they had come. "As you know," they said, "our good old troll king is gone. And now all the big and small trolls and tomtes and goblins and sprites in the world need a new king. The throne is waiting for him in Seven Mile Mountain. But we don't know who to choose, so we ask your help. Who shall be king of the trolls and lord of Seven Mile Mountain?"

Uggle-Guggle, the witch in the wild forest who was wiser than anyone under the stars, hesitated. She sat down in a dark corner of her cottage, opened her big book of wisdom, put glasses on her nose, and began to mumble some very mysterious words. No one dared interrupt her, and a few minutes of solemn silence passed, broken only by the old crone's murmurs.

At last she rose. All were eagerly awaiting what she would say — the messengers in the cottage, Bull up in the attic, Drull down in the cellar, Klampe-Lampe over in the oven, and Trampe-Rampe out in the shed. They pricked up their ears so as not to miss a word.

"So speaks Uggle-Guggle," she began, "and this I have read in the book of wisdom. What I know, I know, and what I know is my secret. Many have turned their eyes to the throne on Seven Mile Mountain, and many would like to be king of the trolls. One is up there, and one is down there, one is in there and one is out there, and there are still others too, big and small, trolls and tomtes. Still, what

I know, I know, and what I know is my secret, and no one will become the king of the trolls, master of Seven Mile Mountain and lord of the big and small trolls, tomtes and goblins, who cannot always keep his head. The throne in Seven Mile Mountain will be occupied in seven days by a new king."

And with this the messengers had to be content. Everyone — big and small trolls, tomtes and goblins — wondered who it was who could always keep his head.

☩ ❦ ☩

The four big trolls were not having a pleasant time in their hiding places. In the oven, Klampe-Lampe was so terribly uncomfortable that his legs fell asleep, but he did not dare even wiggle a toe. Once he took a deep breath and some flour tickled his nose. He fought the sneeze as hard as he could, pinching his nose with his fingers. In the attic, Bull, was suffering too. The floorboards squeaked at the slightest step, and he feared that any minute they would break under his great weight. Drull, in the dark cellar, had bumped against the barrels and buttertubs, and now he did not dare move lest they tumble down and everyone hear. The only one who was still feeling light-hearted was Trampe-Rampe. He did not know the other big trolls were there, and so he clumped in gaily through the back door to talk to the witch again.

Then Klampe-Lampe found it impossible to hold back his sneeze any longer. Had you offered him all the treasure in Seven Mile Mountain, and the troll kingdom to boot, he would still have sneezed. He simply had to. So he sneezed as if he had a giant trumpet at his nose. He also kicked out with both legs, which pushed open the oven door, and out he came.

Bull and Drull completely lost their heads. Bull leapt in the air and when he landed the floorboards gave way, and he crashed downstairs into the arms of Trampe-Rampe. Drull jumped too, and the barrels and buttertubs boomed and clattered around him. Fearing the cottage itself was tumbling down, he flung open the cellar door and raced upstairs.

So there they stood, all four, and gaped at each other with something less than mildness in their eyes. None of them said a word, only slunk home as fast as they could go.

In their dens, they sat down to think. They understood that they were getting in each other's way, and that it was hard not to, and that no one would become king of the trolls in Seven Mile Mountain unless he could always keep his head. That was what the crone Uggle-Guggle had said. But to each one, the most important thing seemed to be how he could get rid of the other three competitors.

☩ ✤ ☩

Over at Steep Mountain, Drulsery-Drull paced his chambers like a caged bear, and thought and thought. Finally he climbed up on his big boulder to look around and caught sight of Bull, who was pulling a net from his fishpond. Drull was so angry that he lost his head again. He grabbed his boulder with his two great hands and threw it with all his might towards Bunner Mountain, to put an end to his rival with one blow. "I'll show you, you Bunner Mountain fool," he muttered between his teeth.

The boulder missed Bull, but it did land in the fishpond with a splash that echoed seventeen miles around and was heard underground, too. All the water spilled out as if it wished to escape; it thundered, roared, and boomed out, swallowing everything in its way. It spread and spread until the whole valley, where thousands of trolls and tomtes lived, was in danger of being flooded. The trolls and tomtes were beside themselves with fear. Bull scratched his head and stamped his foot in anger. His splendid bathing pool and fishpond had been ruined, but there was nothing he could do about it. Again, everyone lost their heads.

The danger was at its greatest when little Peter Pastureman came strolling along the road driving Bull's oxen back from pasture. He realized in a second what had happened, and in the next second knew exactly what was to be done. He told all the trolls to go home and get spades and pickaxes, and then dig a ditch to release the water. A thousand troll arms soon accomplished the task, and the floodwaters poured into the ditch and soon were flowing harmlessly out to sea.

"No one else would ever have thought of that," said the trolls. "He is a real thunderclap of a boy, our Pastureman, even if he is so small."

By now, Bull had realized who had played the trick on him. He had last seen that boulder perched high on Drull's mountain.

"You will pay for this, you Steep Mountain fool," he snorted, and he found himself a boulder even bigger than Drull's. He flung it furiously and watched with wicked joy as it curved through the air. It landed so hard on Steep Mountain that it started a landslide, and the rest of the mountain nearly followed it.

Drull barely escaped with his life and now sat among the ruins of his home not knowing what to do. It was terribly cold. All the icy winds of the slopes played hide-and-seek through the thousand cracks and holes that had been opened by the landslide. Drull had a toothache too, not just a little one, but one such as no troll had ever had since trolls began. Poor Drull began to howl like eleven hundred wolves until trolls for miles around hurried over to find out what was the matter. But Drull would not tell them; he only cried and yelled and kicked. They begged him to be quiet, but in vain. That night, no one within fifty miles slept a wink.

The next morning, Peter Pastureman went to Steep Mountain to take Drull's goats to graze. When he saw what was the matter, he took his scissors, sheared the whole herd, and wrapped some of the soft, fine hair around Drull's head, so the ache went away. Then with the rest of the hair he filled the cracks and crevices in the mountain so that the winds stayed outside. When all this was done, he blew a jolly tune on his reed pipe and led the goats, leaping and jumping in their shorn coats, up to their mountain pasture.

"Drull would never have thought of that," said the trolls. "And none of us, either. But Peter Pastureman always knows what to do, one way or another."

Peace had hardly been restored before the trolls heard loud shouts from the south and saw enormous clouds of smoke billowing up. This time Trampe-Rampe was up to his tricks. He had been wandering about as usual when he caught sight of Klampe-Lampe hauling logs for his thousand-year-old fire. He remembered the unlucky sneeze in the witch's cottage, and his anger got the better of him. He decided to pay back Klampe-Lampe. He knew that the always-burning fire was Klampe-Lampe's dearest possession, and so he swore to extinguish it for good. Trampe-Rampe approached the fire and blew with all the breath in his lungs, but things did not turn out quite as he had hoped.

The fire began to burn more fiercely and so he blew a second time, even harder than before, so hard that all the sparks and burning logs were blown from the hearth and the whole forest caught fire. The blaze spread as if it had wings, and every moment the danger increased.

All the trolls rushed towards the fire and ran here and there, scared out of their wits. Klampe-Lampe himself scampered off in a panic. But once again Peter Pastureman came to the rescue.

Peter Pastureman was grazing Klampe-Lampe's big herd not far off when he saw smoke. He went to look, then like a whirlwind turned back again, gathered his very best horses, harnessed them to a giant plough, and made a wide furrow all around the burning part of the forest — so wide that the fire could not jump it. And so the fire burnt itself out and the rest of the forest was saved.

Everyone, big and little trolls, tomtes and goblins, went to shake Peter Pastureman's hand. "A real thunderclap of a boy you are," they shouted. "Who else would have thought of that?"

Peter Pastureman patted the horses, blew a merry tune on his birchbark horn, and took the herd back to graze again.

It was not long before Klampe-Lampe discovered who had tricked him. Trampe-Rampe had been seen running away. Now Klampe-Lampe could think only of revenge. He went to High Mountain, where he knew Trampe-Rampe often passed, and found him straight away. They attacked each other with thunder and noise until High Mountain shook from top to bottom and the earth trembled. Trolls ran from their caves and caverns, believing the world was cracking open. And what a terrible sight — to see two of the biggest trolls slugging away at each other like savage forest wolves! They rolled around like great balls, kicking up stones and tree roots, and spitting and hissing like dragons. Not even a king in Seven Mile Mountain could have stopped them.

Attempts to separate them were in vain. An old man and woman who lived in a big gorge on High Mountain were the most troubled of all. They were used to the wild roaring of the winter winds that fought on the mountainside, but had never endured a tumult such as this. The old man shouted to them to spare his mountain, but Klampe-Lampe and Trampe-Rampe, in the thick of the fight, neither heard nor cared. They fought all that day and the next too without a moment's pause and without either of them winning or losing. How long the fight might have gone on is difficult to say, had not Peter Pastureman come along.

Peter hurried away to old Whitebeard of Snowfall Mountain and whispered in his ear, his eyes shining with mischief. The old man nodded, and Peter left with Whitebeard's biggest troll sack, which contained a million times a million snowflakes and was used only once every hundred years.

Peter Pastureman came to High Mountain, where Klampe-Lampe and Trampe-Rampe were still rolling around hitting each other. He untied the troll sack and at once, the snowflakes, delighted to be free, whirled out in hundreds and hundreds and thousands and thousands. Soon the two trolls were blinded. They could not see a thing for snowflakes and they had to stop fighting. As they emerged from the clouds of snow, they looked around, shamefaced, at the great crowd of spectators. Both Klampe-Lampe and Trampe-Rampe knew their reputation was in shreds, and without a word they ran away and hid.

The old man and woman of High Mountain took Peter Pastureman's hand and thanked him. "Little Peter Pastureman," they said, "you have more sense than anyone north or south, east or west. You have helped us out of many dangers, and you certainly keep your head."

A murmur went through the crowd of trolls. That was exactly what Uggle-Guggle had said, she who was wiser than anyone under the stars: "No one will become the king of the trolls, master of Seven Mile Mountain and lord of the big and small trolls, tomtes and goblins, who cannot always keep his head."

Had seven days passed since the troll messengers visited the cottage in the densest part of the wild forest? The days were carefully counted, and it was so.

Once again High Mountain was in an uproar, but this time it was a happy noise. Little Peter Pastureman was hoisted on the shoulders of the crowd in triumph, and a long row of dancing, singing trolls wove down to Seven Mile Mountain, where Peter was solemnly placed on the throne. Thousands and thousands of trolls proclaimed him king over mountain and valley, forest and lake.

Thus Peter Pastureman became king of all the trolls. He lived a long and happy life, and it was said of him, "Our king always keeps his head."

To this day, the water from Bull-Bull-Bulsery-Bull's lake flows down that mountainside and around the stone that Drull-Drull-Drulsery-Drull threw in anger. Even today there is a river all the way to the sea where the trolls dug their ditch. Steep Mountain still looks lopsided from the boulder that split it. And hardly a bush grows where Klampe-Lampe's fire burned the forest, while on the top of High Mountain the snow from Whitebeard's troll sack never melts.

Sketch of girls on horseback, led by a youth

BRAVE GIRLS & BOYS

*Much more goes on in children's heads
than grown-ups can ever guess...*

The Yule Goat, for John's son Putte

From *A Knight Rode Forth* by Jeanna Oterdahl

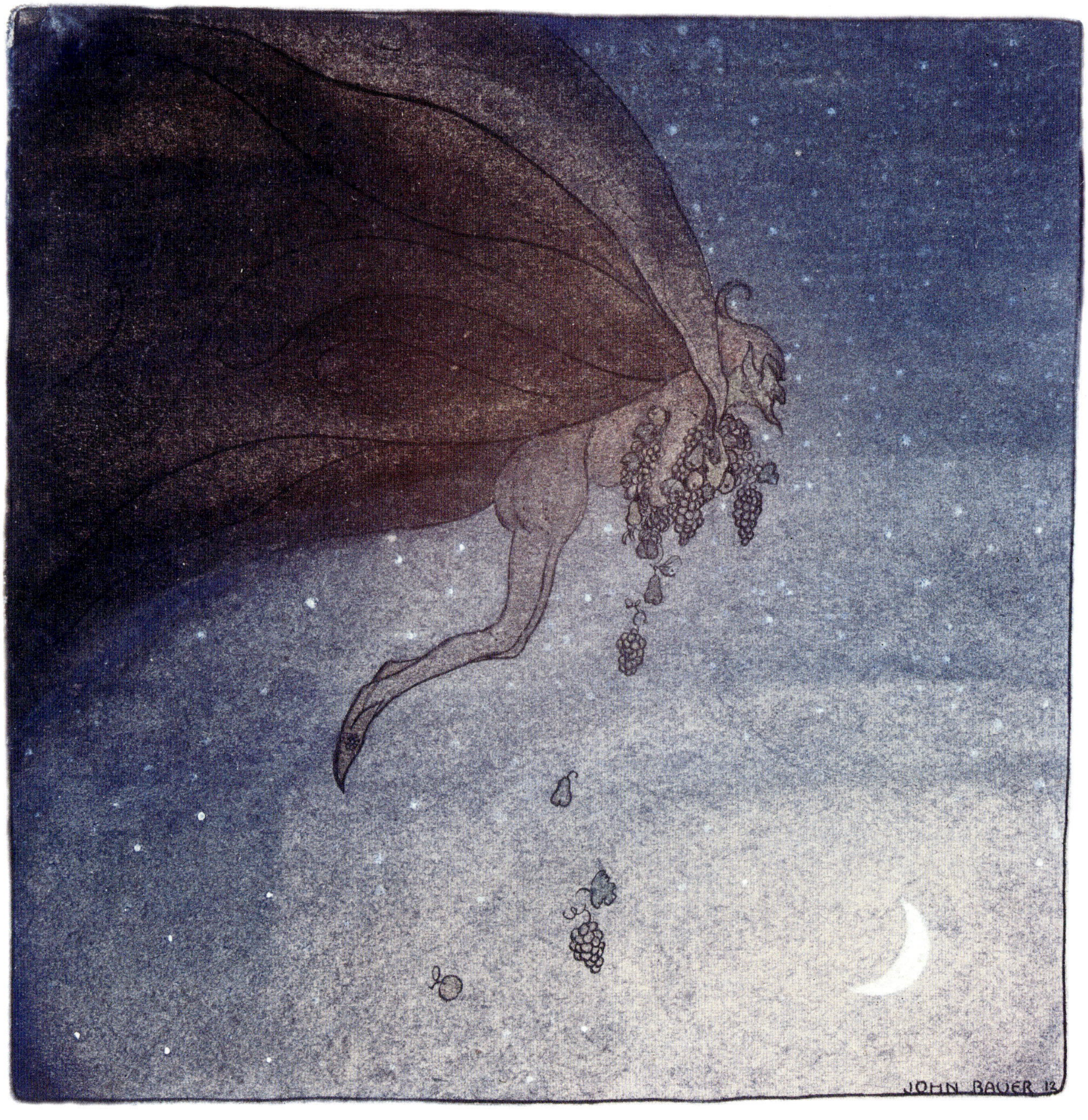
JOHN BAUER 12

The Magician's Cape

Anna Wahlenberg

Once upon a time, a wicked magician built a splendid castle high on a mountain. Between the cliffs in front of the castle he conjured up a wonderful garden, where magnificent flowers glowed, delicious fruits ripened, and the sweetest grapes grew. There the magician would lie on a velvet couch under the branches watching beautiful young girls dance on the lawn, and sing and play the guitar.

The songs were merry, but the dancers themselves looked very sad, because they hated the evil magician who had taken them from their parents. Yet they trembled for their lives, because as soon as the magician thought one of them did not play or dance well enough, he would open the garden gate and push her into the deep forest outside, which was full of bears and wolves. Many dancers never found their way back home again.

Whenever the magician had discarded a girl, he would put on the fine velvet robes of a distinguished gentleman, dab his lips with honey to make words come out sweetly, and drip magic dew in his eyes to make them look gentle and sparkling. Then he would don his black flying cape, which he could change into enormous wings, and fly out to find another victim.

If he saw a girl who pleased him, he would spread his cape at her feet, just as a noble knight would to honor a pretty maiden. And if the girl stepped willingly on to it, he would quickly wrap her up in a corner of the cape and fly away with her. Should she ignore him, however, he could not harm her, for he only had power over those who stepped on his cape of their own free will.

During one of his flights, he came to a small village and saw a smith's daughter, Alvida, sitting at a window combing her long yellow hair.

Her face was so serene and her eyes were so clear that the magician was delighted at the sight of her. He watched and waited until he saw her come outside with a basket on her arm and walk towards the forest to pick berries. Then he slipped ahead of her, and where the forest path turned off, he suddenly stepped out and spread his black cape before her.

"Beautiful maiden," he said, "your feet are so small and fine they ought not to touch the ground. Step on my cape!"

At first Alvida was frightened, but then she laughed. "I am no beautiful maiden. And really, you ought to take better care of your handsome cape. Imagine dropping it in the middle of the path: it will be covered with mud and pine needles!" She picked up the cape, carefully shook it out, and returned it to the magician. "Now, that's better. Don't do it again, though, for it would be a great pity to ruin such a fine cape." She scolded him with her finger, nodded, and skipped into the forest.

But the magician so wanted to take her back to his castle that he followed stealthily, wondering how to catch her.

Then he saw a herd of goats grazing in a dell, and among them an enormous ram with curved horns. If I could make that ram frighten her, he thought, then I could hold out my cape to protect her. She would hide behind it and step on to it.

Taking out a magic whistle, the magician blew on it and attracted a swarm of bees and hornets, which stung the ram to a frenzy. It tried to butt the bees with its horns, and when that did not work, it looked around for something else to butt. It caught sight of Alvida and rushed full tilt towards her, exactly as the magician had hoped. In two quick steps, the magician was at Alvida's side holding up his cape as if to protect her from the onrushing ram.

But although Alvida was frightened by the ram, she did not seek safety behind the magician's cape. Instead, she ran behind a pine tree, where she and the ram chased each other round and round.

When she tripped over a root, the magician quickly spread his cape, hoping she would fall on it. But it was the ram that streaked in and entangled its horns in the magician's cape. The magician knocked it senseless, and when he freed the sharp horns, much to his annoyance he saw that his cape had a big tear in it.

Alvida, feeling that she had caused the magician's accident, felt very sorry for him and walked towards him. "What a pity that your beautiful cape is torn," she said. "Perhaps I can mend the tear."

She picked a thorn from a rose bush, and with another thorn pierced the first at the top to make a sewing needle. Then she plucked a thin strand of her yellow hair to use as a thread.

"Give me your cape," she urged. "If I stitch it neatly I don't think you will see the tear, and when you get home someone else can repair it properly." She folded the cape over her knee and sewed up the rip as well as she could.

"Just let me see if it will do." The magician held the cape up to the light and shook his head: she must make a few more stitches.

With her needle in hand, Alvida took a step towards the magician and reached for the cape. At the same moment, the magician lowered the cape and dragged it on the ground. Alvida put her foot on the hem, and in a second the magician had wrapped her up in that corner. Full of anguish, Alvida saw the cape turn into a pair of enormous wings and felt herself being carried aloft.

But more terrible than this was the way the magician's face changed. His eyes became rolling balls of fire; his mouth opened in a grin and terrible tigerish fangs jutted forth.

"Help, help!" Alvida cried in terror.

And as if her cry had been heard, the strand of yellow hair with which the tear in the cape had been sewn caught on a high branch of the pine tree. No matter how the magician pulled and tugged, the strand was so strong it did not break, and while he was pulling and tugging, the cape became entangled among the leaves and branches. To free it, the magician had to let go of Alvida's waist. Quickly, she slipped from him on to a lower branch and jumped to the ground.

She ran home as fast as she had ever run in her life, and once she was inside, fell on the floor in fear and exhaustion. It was a long while before she recovered enough to tell her father and mother what had happened.

The magician flew back to his castle so full of rage that everyone within hid for fear of his anger. No one dared speak or even whisper until he had shut himself up in his room.

He lay on the bed and closed his eyes but could not sleep. His room seemed to him unusually light. The moon must be shining through the window, he thought, and rolled over.

Still the light was so bright he could not sleep. He rose to close the shutters, and when he looked out he saw that there was no moon in the sky. Turning round, he realized that the light was coming from the flying cape, which he had hung over a chair: it came from the seam sewn with Alvida's yellow hair, which shone out as brightly against the dark cloth as a good deed shines against an evil one.

Well, that is easily taken care of, he thought. He rolled the cape up tightly so that the seam was inside, and climbed back into bed. But he had hardly closed his eyes before the radiance filled the room again. The golden seam was shining right through all the folds of the cape.

Angrily, the magician rushed forward with a knife and cut the seam from the cape, leaving a large hole, and then he threw the golden threads out of the window.

Now I shall be free to sleep, he thought.

But no sooner had he closed his eyes again than once more he sprang up in a rage. The light was there again. He examined the cape and found that the seam had reappeared, shining brightly.

The magician carried the cape to the deepest, darkest cellar in the mountain, but it was no use. As soon as he lay down on his bed again, brightness filled the room. It shone through walls, floor and ceiling, and eventually he realized that he would never be able to escape its light.

☩ ✿ ☩

He did not sleep a wink that night, or the next, or the next. As the fourth night approached, he threw his flying cape over his shoulders and flew down to the little village where Alvida lived. He rapped on her window.

"Who is it?" she asked, sitting up in bed, startled from sleep.

"It is me," he said. "Open your window so I can talk to you. I will not hurt you."

But Alvida had recognized the magician's voice, and hid silent and shivering under her blanket.

"Come here," he urged. "Your wicked yellow hair, with which you sewed my cape, keeps shining and won't let me sleep. Undo that seam or I will make you suffer."

But he could not frighten Alvida now, for she remembered that trolls and magicians never dare to force their way into Christian homes. So Alvida lay still, as if nothing had happened.

The magician began to beg. "If you undo the seam, I will give you a sack of gold."

Alvida did not move.

"If you cut the seam, you can have a big farm with fields and pastures."

Regardless of the wonderful things he offered, Alvida would not answer. In the end, the magician had to return to his castle having accomplished nothing. Yet as he entered the castle garden, he had an idea. He could not bribe Alvida, but if he could give her something, perhaps the gift would make her grateful and she would agree to cut away the shining seam.

So he bent down the branches of the trees in his garden and picked the most luscious fruits, pulled up the grape vines with their heavy bunches, swept them all in his cape, and flew back to Alvida's window. There he planted the grape vines, arranged them over the wall, fastened them to the windowsill and the roof beams, and hung all the fruit he had picked among the bunches of grapes, so that a beautiful border now framed the small window.

The magician flew back to his castle and went to bed. And the strange thing was that this time when he closed his eyes, the golden thread shone only faintly and he could go to sleep.

☩ ✤ ☩

Alvida looked out of her window the next morning, and her eyes fell on a poor old woman sitting by the ditch eating a big juicy pear. The old woman stood and curtsied.

"Thank you for the beautiful pear," she said. "It fell from your window to the highway, and fruit that lies on the highway is for anyone to take."

When Alvida saw how handsomely her window had been decorated, she realized that the magician was trying to persuade her to rip out the shining thread.

Alvida did not touch any of the fruit herself. She let it fall, piece by piece, and tired and thirsty travelers came along, picked up a pear or an apple, and blessed the gift. Every evening the vines were bare, but by morning they were full of the most delicious fruit once again.

One night, the magician knocked at Alvida's window again. "Listen, my girl," he said. "I have given you all the treasures of my garden, because it dims the radiance of your foolish seam. But there must come an end to this. Won't you now cut the shining seam from my cape so that I may finally sleep in peace?"

But Alvida did not answer. She thought the seam was all right where it was.

And the magician never did get rid of it. Every night, he — who only wanted to do evil — was obliged to fly away with gifts for the tired and unhappy. And if he ever dared carry off a maiden, no matter how fancifully he decorated Alvida's window the golden seam shone so blindingly both day and night that the magician did not get a moment's peace until he had taken her home again where she belonged.

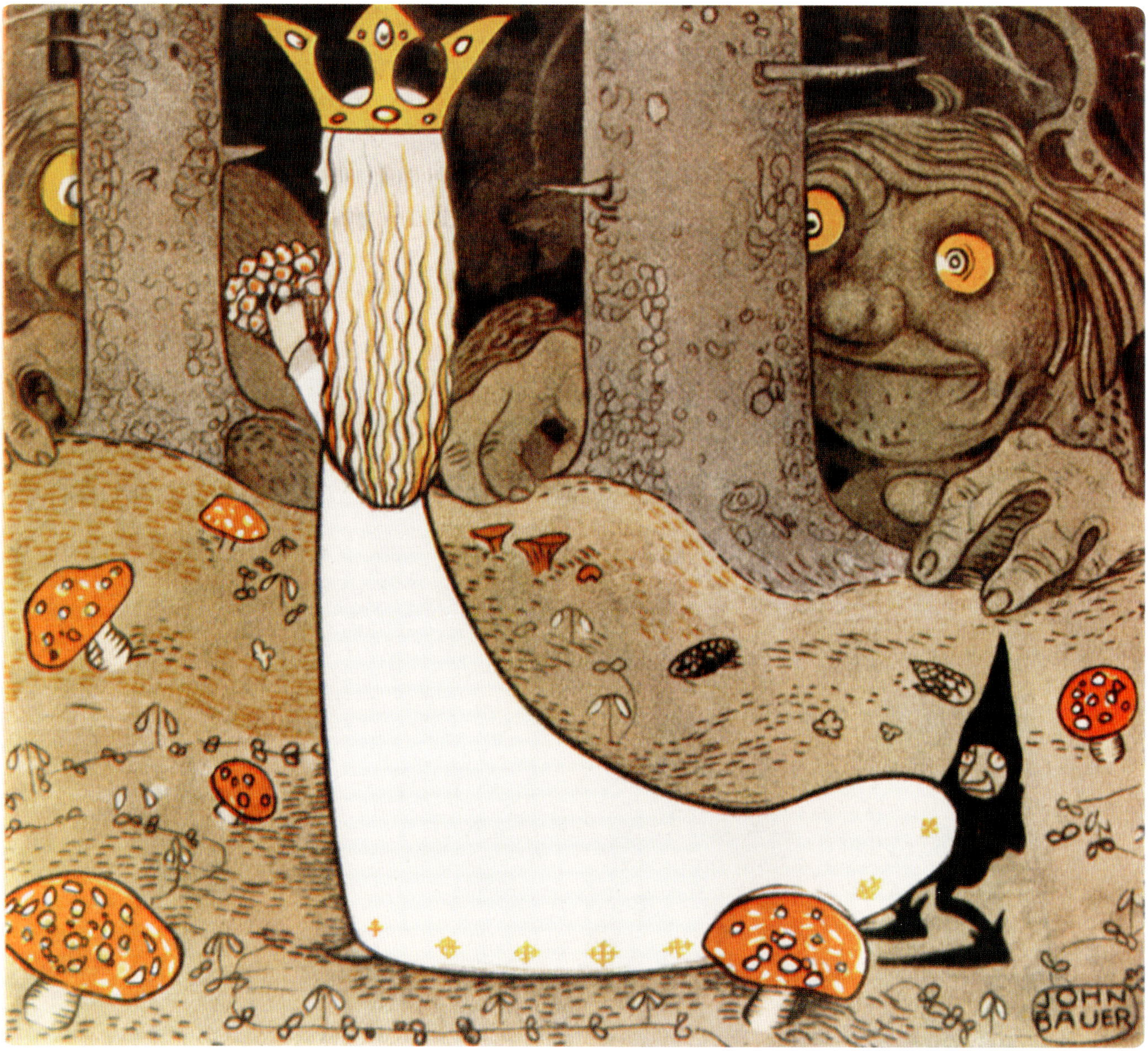
JOHN
BAUER

Dag, Daga and the Flying Troll of Sky Mountain

Harald Östenson

After their parents passed away, Dag and Daga lived all by themselves in their little forest cottage. The loving brother and sister picked themselves up from their misfortune and swore to look after each other as best they could. They tended their goats, which gave them plenty of milk, and picked mushrooms and berries, which the boy Dag sometimes exchanged for a little flour.

The girl Daga cooked porridge and baked bread as her mother had done, although she was very young. Dag was as skilful with a bow and arrow as his father had once been, and since in those days no one worried about poachers, he was able to get all the wild game they needed. Some days Dag would return with a hare or grouse, and once or twice he even brought home a deer, so they did not go hungry.

The brother and sister lived like this year after year, helping each other in every way they could.

But one day Dag did not return from hunting, though Daga waited up for him all evening and all night. The next morning she went out to look for her brother. She knew the direction he had set off in, but that was all.

About midday she came upon a bank of wild roses and suddenly she gave a happy shout. Dag must be in there, for she could see the feather of his cap, which she herself had sewn on, sticking out of the bushes. She ran up, full of hope. But when she came nearer, she saw that the cap was hanging all by itself on a high branch.

A little farther on she caught sight of Dag's bow and arrows, but there was no sign of him. She tried in vain to break through the thorns, but the wild roses grew so thickly that it was quite impossible for her to get any nearer to his things. "How could he have got in there?" Daga wondered. She went home for an axe, and when at last she cut through and held her brother's belongings in her hands, night had fallen.

The next morning Daga rose early. She put food in a bundle, took up a walking stick, and let the goats out to graze. They would have to look after themselves as best they could while she looked for Dag. She walked to their nearest neighbors, a long way, and when she finally reached them they could not help her.

"If he has run into mischief, you won't be able to find him for you are only a girl," they said. "You should leave him to his fate and come and work for us. We could give you food and lodgings. If you go out to find him, you will probably get lost, too."

Of course Daga realized it might be dangerous, but she could not leave her brother to his fate. So she said goodbye and went on her way.

She walked through great forests and over high mountains, and was often so tired that her legs collapsed under her. Then she would rest awhile and trudge on. She spent many nights on beds of moss under sheltering fir trees, and was terrified that wild animals would come and eat her up, but they never did.

And do you know why? Because Daga was never as alone as she thought she was. If she had looked really carefully behind her, she would have seen someone following. It was a tiny old man with a wrinkled face who had followed her when she left the cottage in the woods. He was the tomte of their little cottage, as you may have guessed, and when she fell asleep on the forest floor, he kept watch beside her. If a wolf or any wild beast approached, he stared at it hard until it ran away.

One day, after Daga had walked several hours, she sat down to rest on a moss-covered stone. Around her, the forest was fresh with dew. The chaffinches in the tops of the pine trees were singing happily, and would have made her happy if she had not felt so sad.

Suddenly she heard the sound of dogs barking, and soon a handsome prince in splendid hunting costume walked towards her. When he saw her he stood still, looking at her for a moment, then he called his attendants, who had by now caught up with him.

"Look! A beautiful princess," he exclaimed. "I will ask her to be my bride. Hurry back to the palace, fetch a sedan chair and bring her there."

Hearing this, Daga fell on her knees before the prince and pleaded, "Let me go, my lord. I must find my brother, who has been stolen away. I cannot be your bride, for I am merely the daughter of a poor hunter."

The prince only answered, "Please come. My servants will find your brother for you."

In a little while the sedan chair arrived, and Daga reluctantly agreed to accompany the prince, in hope that his men would be able to find Dag. She was escorted into a chamber at the palace, and the ladies-in-waiting dressed her in a magnificent white gown. Then the prince placed a crown of gold on her head and golden bands on her arms.

"These are welcoming gifts," he said. "You may keep them even if you decide not to become my bride."

He then led her into a large hall crowded with noblemen and ladies. All evening she sat by his side, and he was as courteous and attentive to her as if she had been a real princess.

But as Daga returned to her bedchamber after the banquet, she overheard two valets talking in a dark corridor.

"Can you imagine it, seven of us have to look for a hunter who's disappeared in the forest," said one.

"Don't worry," replied the other. "Just have a good time for a few days, then come back and say you couldn't find him."

"Well, how could we find him, anyway? The trolls have probably caught him."

You may imagine how Daga felt when she heard this.

As soon as she reached her chamber, she quickly gathered her belongings together, tied them in a little bundle, and slipped from the castle so quietly that no one saw or heard her. It was night, but she could not have slept peacefully in a beautiful bedchamber knowing that no one was doing anything to find her brother.

She still wore the white gown and the golden crown on her head as she walked sadly under the dark pine trees. The little tomte from the forest cottage followed behind. He had been welcomed by the palace tomte, who had given him a velvet suit and pointed shoes, but when Daga left the castle, he too had to go.

It grew darker and darker, and then Daga caught sight of two monstrous trolls creeping towards her between the trees. They had round eyes that shone like fireflies and enormous hands that seemed ready to clutch whatever came close. Daga was terrified, but she did not return to the safety of the palace. The trolls came closer, then stopped, as if they had seen something behind her, something that frightened them. Daga hurried away.

At daybreak, Daga sat down to rest. By now she was far from the castle, hidden by dense undergrowth, and was sure no one could find her and make her go back. At last she stopped to take off her golden crown, the golden bands on her arms, and the white gown. She packed them all in her bundle and put on her old clothes again.

She walked all day until, towards evening, she met a little girl. It was hard to tell whether she was a troll or a human, but Daga decided she looked like a girl.

As always when she met someone, Daga spoke of her lost brother and asked advice about how to find him.

"Give me a gown fit for a princess," sneered the girl, "and I'll tell you who caught your brother." She looked disdainfully at Daga's plain dress.

"But I *can* give you a princess's gown," said Daga, and she took out the white dress the prince had given her.

The little girl was plainly taken by surprise. She wanted to go back on her promise, but she could not. "The Flying Troll of Sky Mountain caught your brother," she burst out angrily. "And if you go to Sky Mountain, you too will be caught." Then she snatched the gown and ran off.

"The Flying Troll of Sky Mountain," Daga said to herself, and after that, all she could think of was how to get to Sky Mountain.

For seven weeks she wandered until at last the mountain loomed ahead of her, high as the sky, steep and awesome. At the summit she could see the turrets and battlements of a dark, gloomy castle.

For three long days Daga walked around the foot of the mountain, trying to find a place to begin climbing. But the mountain rose as sheer as a wall, and seemed impossible to climb.

On the evening of the third day she met a surly dwarf. "Good evening, little Father," she said. "Can you tell me where to begin climbing the mountain?"

"Certainly," said the dwarf with a mocking laugh, "if you'll just give me two heavy gold bands for my trouble." And he laughed again.

"Here you are," said Daga, pulling forth the golden arm bands the prince had given her.

Abruptly the dwarf stopped laughing and seemed both surprised and angry. But he had to keep his promise, so he took Daga to a place where a crevice zigzagged all the way up the mountainside.

"If you are strong and agile and don't get dizzy, you can probably climb up here," he said. "I expect, however, that you'll fall and break your neck." And he went on his way.

As soon as the sun rose the next morning, Daga began to climb the mountain by stepping on to little ledges and outcrops and hanging on with her hands. It was difficult, dangerous, and tiring. Here and there, however, the crevice leveled out so she could sit and rest, or even lie down for a little while. If she was careless she would fall into the abyss, so she tried not to look down and not to become dizzy. She climbed for nine days until at last she reached the top of the mountain.

The path that led to the troll castle wound among jagged rocks overhung with boulders that seemed ready to fall at any moment. She was trudging along this path when suddenly she heard a loud shout.

Her brother's head thrust up from among the rocks. His face was pale, but he was alive.

"Run, dear sister! Run!" he called.

"I have not walked a hundred miles through the forest and climbed a sky-high mountain to run away just when I find you," his sister answered. "I have come to help you."

"You cannot," said her brother. "All that awaits you here is terrible imprisonment. The troll flew me here and wanted me to hammer gold for him like a slave. When I neither could nor would, he cast a spell on me. My whole body is trapped in this stone. I can only move my head a little."

Daga covered her face with her hands and wept bitterly, but after a while she hurried on towards the castle.

Inside the castle, sitting on a high golden throne, was the terrible Flying Troll. All around him, goblins and sprites were busy hammering and forging gold. When Daga entered, they were so surprised they all dropped their tools.

"Please, Flying Troll," said Daga, "don't keep my brother in that rock any longer. Let him come home with me."

"Did you really believe that if you climbed all the way up here to beg me to free him, I would?" asked the troll. "You are too foolish for words. But if, before I count three, you give me a solid gold crown fit for a queen, you and your brother may leave in peace. If you don't give one to me, I'll throw you higher than you can see and let you fall to the ground in front of your brother's nose."

When the troll had finished speaking, he and the goblins began to laugh so uproariously that you could have thrown half an ox into their ugly mouths. The Flying Troll began to count, and as he said 'two,' Daga threw the golden crown into his black claw.

You can imagine how baffled the trolls and goblins were, but the Flying Troll had to keep his word, no matter how angry he was, and soon Dag and Daga were happily on their way home.

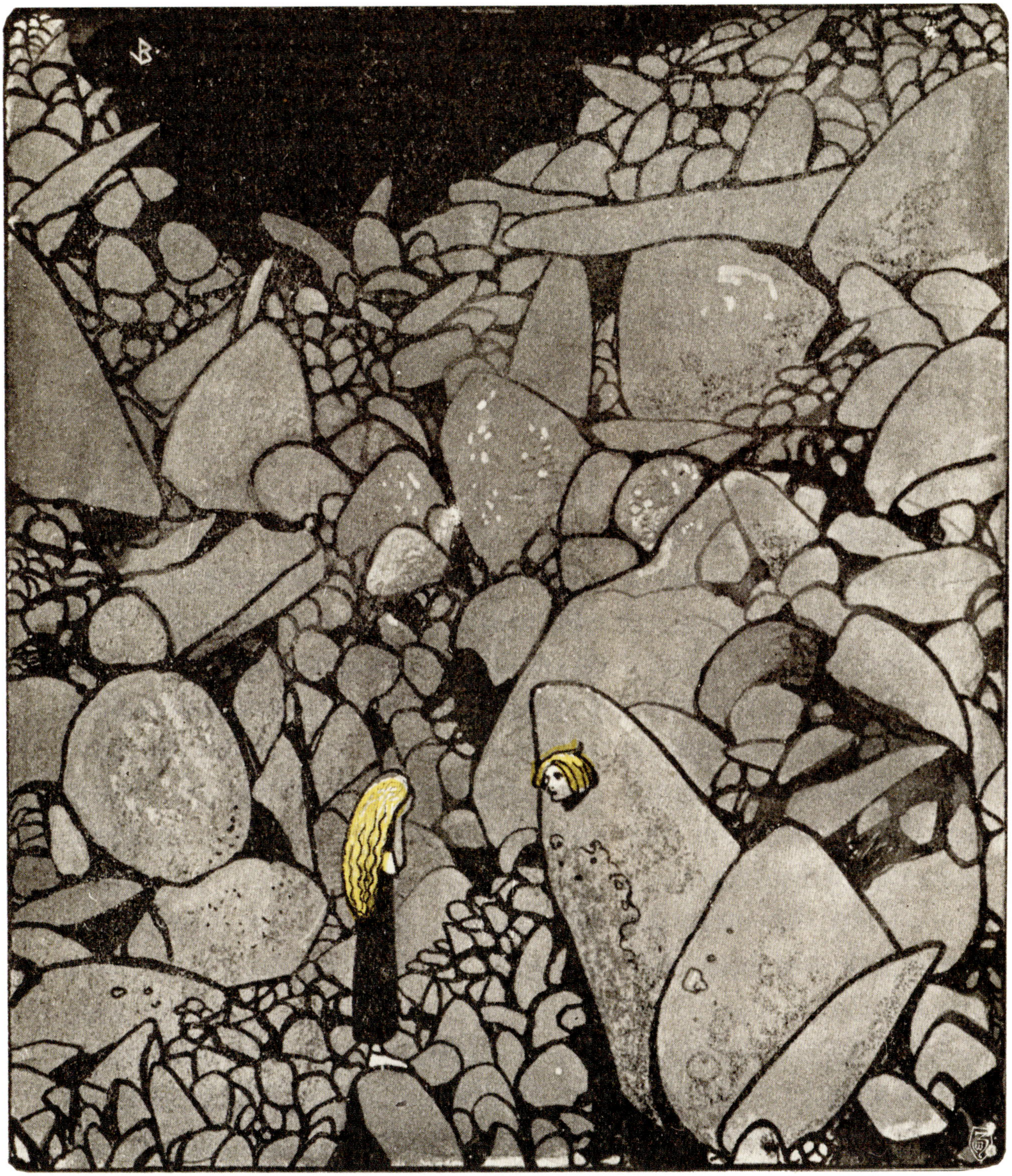

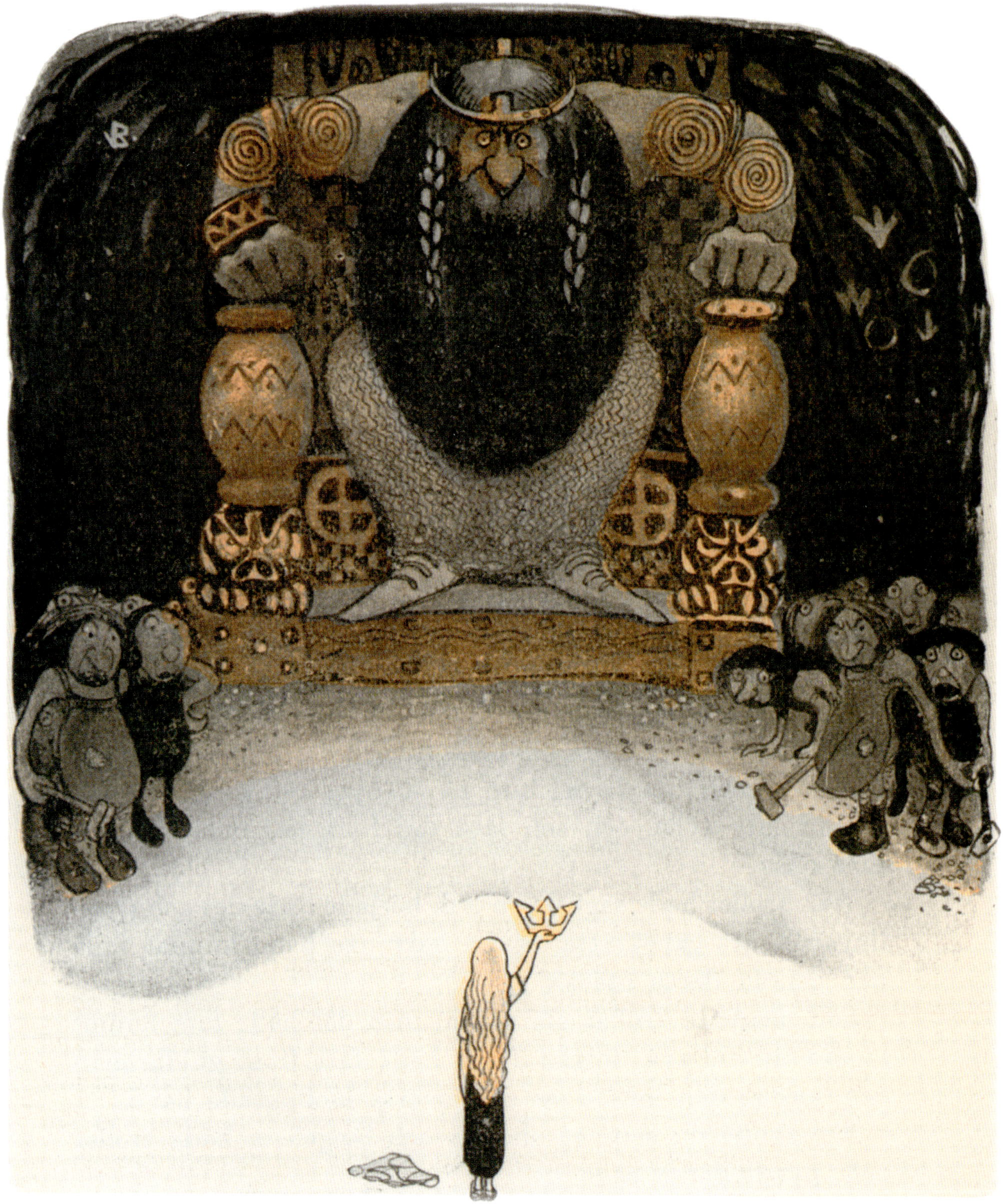

But the merry prince of the castle had not forgotten the girl he met in the forest. He understood why she had left him, for the lady-in-waiting who escorted Daga to her bedchamber had told him what Daga had overheard. First he punished his false valets, and then he himself set out to look for Daga. At last he found her, long after she and her brother had returned to their little cottage.

The prince learned what a faithful and courageous sister she had been, and he fell even more deeply in love with her. When he asked Daga to be his bride, this time she said yes.

So Daga and the prince married and were very happy together, and Dag was always welcomed warmly when he visited his brave sister at the palace.

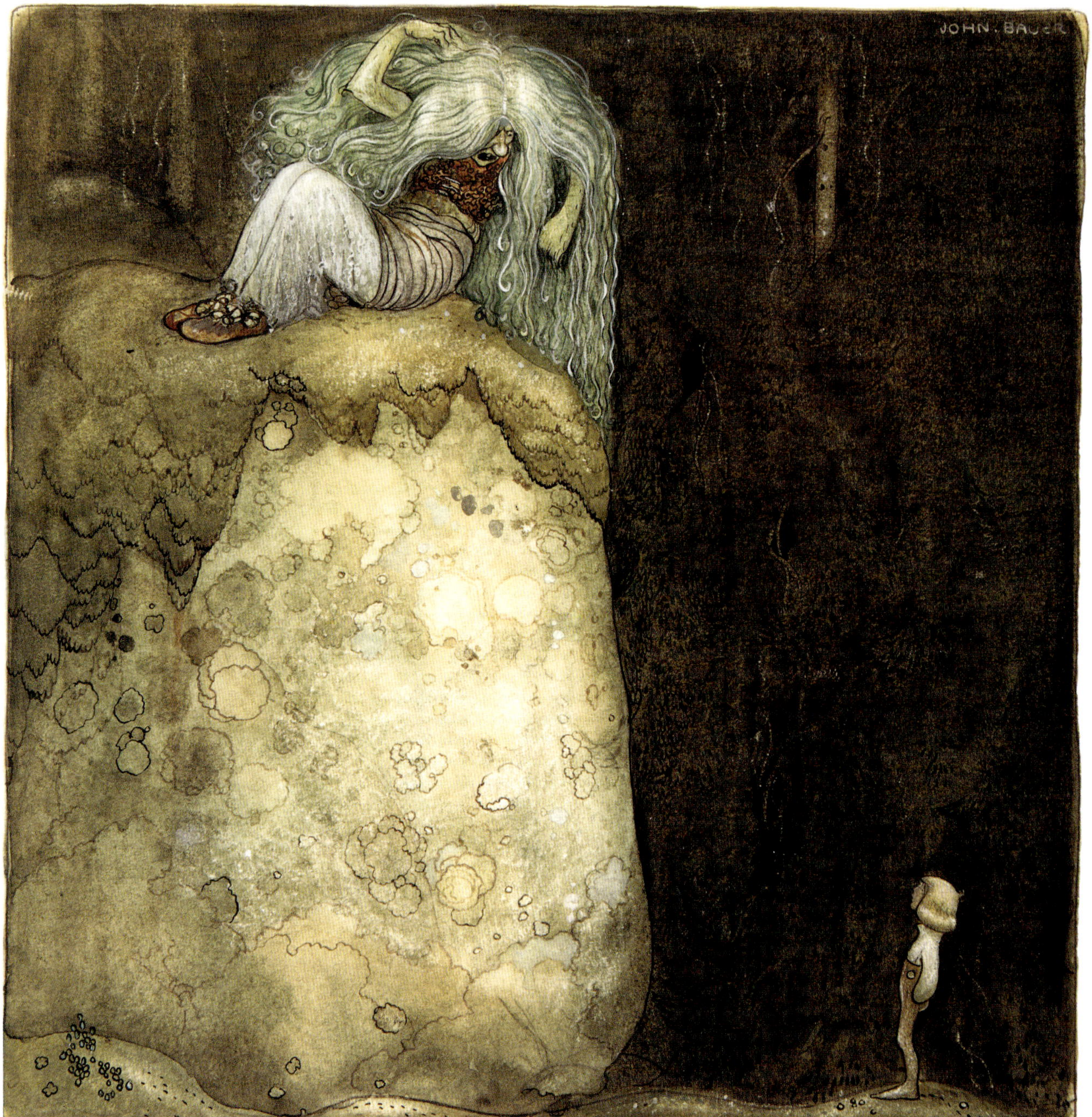
JOHN. BAUER

The Boy Who Was Never Afraid

Alfred Smedberg

Once there lived a poor crofter with eight hungry children and only one cow. Yet the cow, Lily White, was a great blessing to the crofter. She gave as much milk as the finest manor-house cow, which was lucky, considering all those children. She was big and handsome, and clever, too. She understood everything the children chattered about, and they chattered night and day.

Words cannot tell how kind and devoted the children were to Lily White. She was just a cow on a croft, yet she was happy as a bird on the wing. In summertime she grazed in a large pasture by the manor house, but when the sun went down she always managed to come home by herself, because she was so clever.

But one evening, Lily White did not return as usual. The crofter spent half the night looking for her, but came home alone and tired.

At daybreak the next morning, he and his wife and the elder children went to look for their cow in the pasture. At last, in a far corner of the field, they found Lily White's hoofprints in the soft earth. Beside them were others, made by big, clumsy feet. The crofter was frightened, for he realized at once whose footprints they were: none other than the big troll in Hulta Wood.

The troll must have come down to the pasture from his caves in the granite mountain and led the cow away with him.

The children cried, and their father and mother were so worried they scarcely said a word. It was out of the question to try to get the cow back, for no one had ever dared enter the terrible mountain caves where the trolls lived.

There were not only trolls to be frightened of in the deep, haunted Hulta Wood; there were three other creatures too, nearly as dangerous. The first was the green-haired witch; the second was the bellowing watchdog; and the third was a bear, the shaggy king of the forest.

☩ ❦ ☩

Now it happened that among the crofter's children was one small red-cheeked boy named Nisse. As soon as Nisse learned what had happened to Lily White, he immediately decided to walk to the troll caves and bring her back. His mother and father let him go, for they knew there was no one like Nisse in seven parishes. He wasn't afraid of anything in the world, no matter how dangerous it was. Nisse was not afraid because he was so good-hearted and friendly towards every living thing.

Nisse took a stick in his hand, put a slice of buttered bread in his pocket, and set out. Soon he arrived at the forest and after a while he caught sight of a witch sitting on a ledge combing her tousled green hair, which fell all the way down to her hips. It was the quick-footed witch of Hulta Wood.

"What are you doing here in my forest?" she called, as Nisse came walking along.

"I'm looking for our cow, dear lady. The trolls have stolen her," replied Nisse without stopping.

"Now wait a minute, you," the witch screamed, and she jumped down from the ledge to grab his collar.

But at that moment her long hair caught in the spreading branches of a fir tree, and she was left hanging, the tips of her toes just above the ground, and could not get free. She began to kick and twist and shout as loud as she could. Anyone else would have laughed and said it served her right, but Nisse was not like that.

"Tch, tch, little Mother," he said in a friendly voice. "I'll help you."

So he climbed up the tree, pulled and loosened the thick tufts of hair, and at last managed to free the witch from the heavy branches.

"You're an odd one, to help someone who wants to hurt you," said the witch in surprise. "I intended to give you a thrashing, but now I might help you instead."

"That would be good of you, little Mother," said Nisse.

"You'll never be able to get past all the dangerous animals here unless you know their language," said the witch. "But I will give you a magic herb. If you put it in your ear, you will understand everything they say while you are in the forest."

Nisse thanked the witch, did as she told him, and walked on.

☩ ✺ ☩

After he had gone some way, he came to the great angry watchdog of the forest. It limped towards him on three legs and made a fierce face.

"Poor little doggy," said Nisse, full of confidence and sympathy. "Have you hurt yourself? Can I help you?"

The dog had been ready to jump on the boy, but was so surprised by his kindness that it sat down on its hind legs just like a well-behaved dog. "You're not like other people, are you?" it said.

"Perhaps not," said the boy. "Let me see your paw, little Father."

The dog gave him its forepaw, and Nisse saw there was a big thorn in it. He pulled the thorn out, put a little wet moss on the wound, and tied it together neatly with grass.

"That feels better," said the watchdog, standing on all fours. "I had intended to bite your ears, but I don't want to now. Where are you going?"

"Our cow is lost," Nisse replied. "I am going to the troll caves to find her."

"My, my!" said the watchdog with a pitying look. "That is not an easy errand, for those trolls are not to be trifled with. But since you were kind enough to cure my foot, I'll go with you and show you the way. Perhaps I can help you."

The watchdog did as it had promised. It leapt ahead, and the boy scampered after it, and then they went deep, deep into the forest. They had run for several hours when they caught sight of the bear lumbering through a peat bog, sniffing for cranberries.

"You had better go round," said the watchdog, "for he attacks people and cattle."

"Well, I like the way he looks, even if he is big and shaggy," said the boy, and kept on walking.

Just then the bear saw him. It rose on its hind legs, let out a terrible growl, and padded towards him.

"My, what a great rough voice you have," said the boy, putting out his small hand in greeting. "You would make a fine bass in a choir."

"Uff," grunted the bear, stepping closer.

"Yes, a very loud voice," continued the boy. "But you seem very friendly, anyway, holding up both paws to greet me."

The bear was just about to gobble Nisse up, when the green-haired witch jumped out from the trees. She had followed Nisse at a distance to see what would happen to him in the troll caves.

"Don't touch that boy," she cried to the bear and she picked up a knotted fir stump and flung it into the bear's wide-open mouth. The stump stuck between its jaws so that it could neither growl nor bite.

"That was a mean thing to do to old Father here, who was so friendly and wanted to greet me with both his paws," said the boy. "But wait, let's see if I can't help you out of this."

He found a long wooden stick and began poking it into the bear's mouth. The bear sat still, panting, and after much picking and prodding, Nisse at last managed to loosen the stump.

"That was well done," grunted the bear contentedly. "I can see you are a boy with pluck and nerve. I was going to swallow you in one gulp, but now you are safe from me for the rest of your life. What are you doing here in the forest?"

"I am looking for our cow. The trolls stole her," Nisse replied.

"Humph, you are a daring boy to set out on an errand like that," said the bear. "I think I'll follow you and perhaps I may be of help."

They all set off again and arrived at the trolls' mountain caves as the sky began to darken. The entrance was covered by mighty boulders, but there was a small opening just about big enough for a dog to squeeze through.

"Nisse can crawl in there," said the bear, adding, "If the troll attacks you, just call 'Bear, come in,' and then the trolls will have a real fight on their hands, I can promise you."

"I don't think it will be necessary," said Nisse, "but thank you just the same."

And so he crawled through the narrow opening and entered a cave as big as a barn. The old troll was sitting by a fire, munching on a bone. He looked awful, with an enormous nose, hairy arms, and yellow-green cat's eyes. And there in one corner of the cave was Lily White, chewing on some rough thistles the troll had picked for her in the forest.

"Why, look, a little urchin!" exclaimed the troll, and grabbing Nisse around the waist, he lifted him to the table. "Where do you come from?"

"Dear friend troll," said Nisse politely. "I have come to fetch our cow, who seems to have wandered into your cave."

"Don't be so foolish," clucked the troll. "Oh no, my little fellow. I needed milk, you see, and so did my old woman. And you yourself will make a fine little chop for our dinner. As soon as Mother returns, she'll put the pan on the fire."

"Oh, you're joking," said Nisse. "You wouldn't be so cruel to a little boy who never did you any harm."

"What nonsense!" cried the troll. "Of course I'll fry you. Aren't you frightened?"

"No, I'm not afraid of you," said Nisse boldly. "I know you're not as bad as you pretend."

"I've never seen the likes of you in my life," growled the troll. "Mother, Mother, come here quick and light the fire!"

A troll woman rushed into the cave and started rubbing flint and steel together to make a fire.

"It's good of you, Little Mother, to make a fire to warm your old man," said Nisse happily. "But now I think it's time for Lily White and me to go home."

But then the old troll caught hold of Nisse and prepared to fling him into the frying pan.

Now most creatures, it is true, can be won over by friendliness, kindness, and generosity, but only force helps with a troll. Nisse realized this now, and so he called, "Bear, come in! Bear, come in!"

You should have seen what happened next. The bear tossed the boulders at the entrance, left and right, with its great paws. Sparks flew in the air. Then the bear rushed into the cave, and behind it came the witch of the woods and the watchdog.

The bear caught the troll firmly by the neck and flung him on to the floor. The dog dug its teeth into the troll woman's jacket until she fell down with a splash right into the pail by the fire. Meanwhile, the witch of the woods went over to Lily White and loosened the rope with which she was tied.

Nisse lost no time in climbing on Lily White's back. He held tight to her long horns and called, "Thank you all for helping me. Don't be too hard on the trolls." Then he urged Lily White on: "Hurry, dear Lily White! Hurry, dear cow!"

They galloped over tree trunks and stones, through forest and meadow, and were both safe and sound back at the croft by the time the sun came up.

There was much rejoicing at the croft. But back in the cave, the trolls were so frightened by the fact that their own forest friends had helped Nisse — just because he was kind and trusting — that they never dared show their noses in the manor-house pasture again.

From *Vinga's Wreath* by Ellen Lundberg-Nyblom

KINGS & QUEENS

Long, long ago there lived an old king who was rather eccentric...

Illustration for a Christmas book

From *Cinderella*

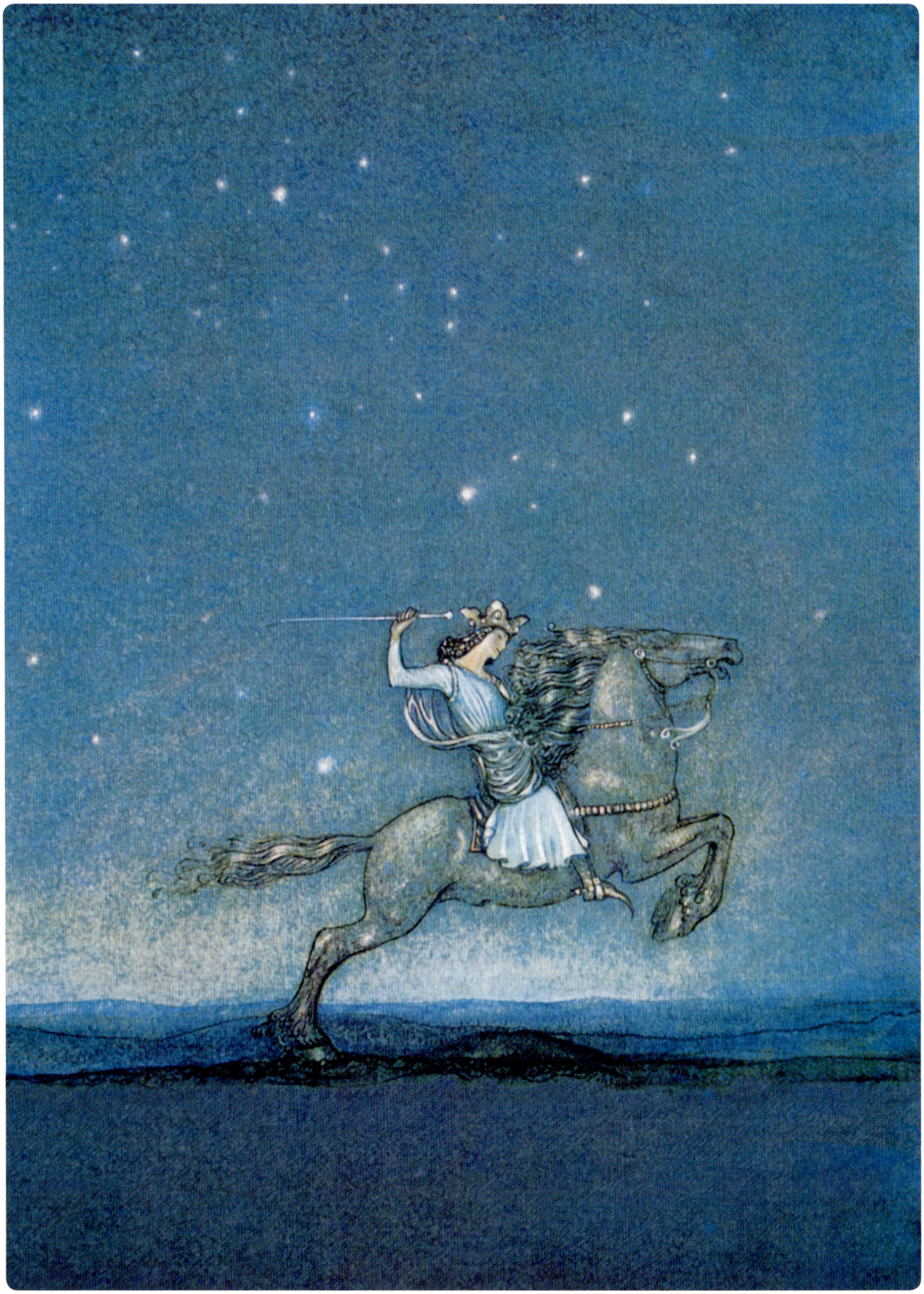

The Ring

Helena Nyblom

Once upon a time, a young prince went riding out in the moonlight. The sky was deep blue, with bright stars floating among wispy clouds. Far away over the mountains, lightning flashed silently. The prince rode quickly, and in the moonlight his shadow looked like a giant ghostly rider.

When the prince reached his castle, he dismounted and gave his horse to a groom. With his riding crop in hand, he walked to the sea and began to stroll slowly along the sandy shore. He was not thinking of anything in particular as he drew deep breaths of the cool night air. Suddenly, the tip of his riding crop caught on something in the sand. What was it?

A ring! thought the prince, and held it up in the moonlight. Who could have lost a ring here by the shore? It must have been one of the ladies-in-waiting. And so the prince tucked the ring in his breast pocket. It was a small ring, slender as a thread, with several little blue stones set to look like a forget-me-not.

The court assembled in the great hall after supper, and the prince put his hand in his breast pocket and said, "Could any of you ladies by chance have lost a ring?"

Immediately all the ladies peered anxiously at their hands and from finger to finger to see if any of their magnificent diamond, emerald, and sapphire rings were missing. But they were all still there.

"What does your ring look like?" one of the ladies dared to ask.

The prince held up the ring.

When the ladies saw it, they all regarded it disdainfully. Certainly none of them would claim such a ring as that; it was a mere trinket, and so small it seemed made for a child's hand.

But now the ladies had something to talk about, and for the rest of the evening they busily compared their beautiful rings, passing them from hand to hand and exclaiming over their cost. The prince rose and strolled to the balcony, where he stood gazing at the moonlight.

Later, he went to his chamber, undressed, and got into bed. He set the little ring on a table near him. Just as he was about to fall asleep, he heard a strange noise, a clicking and whirring as if a small insect were darting among the glasses on the table. When the prince opened his eyes, he was surprised to see that it was the little ring rattling around, as if an unseen hand had set it in motion.

Quickly he lit a candle. Then the ring became still. But as soon as he blew out the candle, the ring began to dance again. It was strange and eerie. The prince put the ring in a drawer, yet he could hear it skittering all night long, and he hardly slept at all. Of course he could have thrown the ring away, but for some reason that seemed to him quite out of the question. He did not wish to part with the ring, and the next night too he brought it to his chamber.

Hardly had he snuffed out the candle than the ring began to dance again, and this time it did not just bounce about the table, but jumped to his chest and bounced just as quickly there.

"What can it mean?" said the prince, and sat up in bed. He caught the ring, jumped out of bed, and put it in a small box, which he locked. As he did so, it seemed to him that the ring quivered and trembled, just as if it were alive.

✠ ❦ ✠

The prince was silent and serious all the next day. He brooded and wondered. What kind of magic ring had he found? That evening, he placed the ring on the table beside his bed as before. He was so tired that he fell asleep at once, but before long he was awakened by something brushing his face. Instantly he realized it was the ring running back and forth over his forehead, dancing down his cheeks, and spinning along his lips.

"I understand!" he exclaimed, and jumped up. "The ring will not leave me alone until I find its owner."

☨ ✣ ☨

Dawn had just begun to break over the sea when the prince went to the stable, saddled his horse, and thundered out across the drawbridge. He rode all day without seeing anyone, but towards evening he arrived at a large castle, beautifully situated in a green meadow surrounded by tall trees. Ivy and roses climbed the walls, and high in an arched window the lady of the castle was standing and looking over the countryside. She was a young and handsome widow who ruled her large estates with a firm hand. When she saw the prince approaching, she dispatched a servant to greet him and welcome him to the castle.

The prince accepted her invitation and gladly went in. The noble lady received him in the friendliest fashion. He was given a splendid chamber, and at dinnertime the large banquet hall was lit with candles and torches, and the table was laid with silver and gold. Servants in festive dress passed around delicious dishes, and the lady herself looked as distinguished as a queen in red velvet and ermine. She talked gaily and seemed highly amused by all the prince had to say. He did not explain why he had ridden there alone, but now and then he cast a quick glance at the lady's hands. Could she have lost the ring?

As it happened, despite this lady's noble birth, she had very large, very red, and very worn hands. She wore many costly rings on her fingers, yet they seemed badly out of place and only showed up her rough hands all the more.

At the end of dinner she peeled an apple for the prince. Looking sharply at her ring-bedecked fingers he asked, "You have so many exquisite rings, my lady. I suppose you could easily lose one bathing or picking flowers?"

"I always take my rings off before I swim in the lake," she laughed. "And I never pick flowers myself. The maids do it for me."

The prince was silent a moment, then he brought forth the little ring and showed it to her. "What do you think of this ring?" he asked.

"That little thing will not fit me," she said, trying to put it on her little finger. "It seems to belong to a child — a poor child. Where did you get it, your highness?"

"That I cannot tell you," the prince answered, and hid the ring in his breast pocket.

The lady's keen black eyes looked searchingly at him for a moment, then she began to talk of other things.

Before dawn, the prince left the castle. *A child,* he thought. *A child — a poor child. But where are you?*

✣ ✤ ✣

He rode through forests and valleys, across meadows and fields, and when the sun was high he came to a large manor house set among waving wheat fields and beautiful flower gardens. Even at a distance he could see many people in a large courtyard. The sound of violins and trumpets reached his ears, and as he came nearer he realized that it was a wedding.

The bride and groom were standing on the front steps. The bride wore a crown of bright ribbons and flowers on her head, and the groom wore a silver-buttoned coat, a glossy black hat, and a happy smile. In the courtyard, a hundred young boys and girls were dancing merrily together. The prince reined in his horse on a small hill not far from the manor house and watched the dancing. When the dancers stopped and sat down to rest on benches in the shade, he rode nearer.

All eyes turned towards the strange rider. The prince held up his little ring and called, "Is there any girl here who has lost a ring?"

The girls flew to him like doves to look at the ring, crowding close and crying:

"I have lost a ring!"

"And I!"

"And I!"

But before long the girls realized that the ring did not belong to any of them, and they all began to babble and chatter, laugh and giggle, and the music started up again. They hurried back to dance, while the prince rode sorrowfully away.

✣ ✤ ✣

He rode on until evening when, feeling tired, he slowed his horse to ride along the bank of a river. Then he caught sight of a woman dressed in black, walking with downcast eyes as though looking for something among the stones by the road. As the prince drew nearer, he saw that the woman was very beautiful, but that the big black eyes in her pale face were full of pain and suffering. He felt very sorry for her.

"Excuse me madam, what are you looking for?" he asked. "Have you lost something precious to you?"

The woman's face became even more melancholy than before. She raised her eyes and her lips trembled. In a quavering voice, she said, "I have lost all I ever had in life: my husband, my estate, my fortune. I had only one thing left: a ring that was a gift from my late husband. I had hoped to sell it well, but now I have lost it and I don't know how or where. And so my last hope is gone. All that is left for me to do is beg my daily bread."

The prince's heart was beating eagerly. Could she be speaking of the ring he was carrying?

Slowly he held up the ring and asked, "Could it possibly be this ring?"

She gave him a sad smile. "My ring was set with a large, costly diamond. That one is nothing in comparison."

Then the prince opened his purse, full of gold coins, and let them rain into the bereaved woman's arms. "This gold may help you for a little while," he said gently. And before the woman had time to thank him, he rode off.

☩ ❀ ☩

He rode for days and nights without encountering anyone who recognized the ring. He always carried it in his breast pocket, and though it no longer danced as it had during the first nights, he could still feel it tugging at him, as if sobbing quietly. The prince heard the small, sorrowful throbbing over the beating of his own heart, and every day he loved the ring more and more.

One morning he came to a swiftly running river. On the opposite bank was a tall mountain, wrapped in the blue veil of early morning mist. All over its slopes sparkled what looked like little gold fires, but they were really broom shrubs in flower, so pretty that the prince could not help feeling happy. He wanted to look at them more closely, but that would not be easy, for there was no bridge over the river.

I suppose I must swim across then, thought the prince, and he and his horse plunged into the rapids. His long, futile search had made him so dejected that he hardly noticed as water sprayed high above him and his horse was almost pulled downstream by the current. At last he stood at the far bank, tired and out of breath, with his horse panting and snorting beside him. The mountain rose before him.

The prince could not climb the slope on horseback, so he let the horse graze while he struggled on foot up a narrow mountain path that wound through a forest towards the summit.

It was a hot day, and the shade of the trees in the cool forest felt refreshing. Everything was still. The sun cast golden flecks over the forest floor. The climbing was not easy, though. *And why am I going to so much trouble?* thought the prince. His heart was beating so violently that he could hear it, and he could also hear the heartthrob of the little ring, pulsing more than it had for a long time.

He paused a moment, then climbed on.

He heard rippling water, and all of a sudden realized how thirsty he was. As he climbed, the sound of the bubbling stream became even stronger, and then he saw something flash white under the leaves of the chestnut trees. Two steps more and he was standing by a fresh mountain spring that was gushing out from a rock wall into a little pool. Then he stood stock still, for he was not alone.

At the spring was a girl, one hand on her hip, watching the water fill her pail; another empty pail was in the grass nearby. She was dressed in a short gray skirt and white blouse, her legs were bare, and her hair hung down her back in two blond braids. The prince could not see her face, but when the pail was full, she turned in his direction. Her blue eyes looked surprised for a moment, but then she bowed her head in greeting and put the second pail under the waterfall. When it was also full, she turned and hooked both pails to a yoke that lay in the grass. The prince smiled at her but she did not smile in return. Her face looked so quiet and serious that suddenly the prince too became serious.

"Forgive me," he said, "but may I have a drink of water? I am so thirsty."

"What will you drink from?" asked the girl. Her voice sounded like soft music. "I know," she said with a quick smile. "Come here. I will help you."

The prince went to the spring, and the girl put her hands together to make a small drinking cup. The water gushed into them and in a second they were full.

"Hurry and drink," she called, and she laughed merrily.

The prince emptied the little cup in a moment. With water still dripping from his mouth, he asked, "More. Please give me one more cup of water."

The girl closed her hands again, and they were filled by the spring. But this time when the prince bent to drink, he noticed a curious change in the girl's face. She blushed, and her eyes, which before had looked as blue as a summer sky, now seemed almost black. She snatched the chain from the prince's neck and seized the ring, which had fallen from his breast pocket when he bent to drink.

"My ring," she said tremulously. "Where did you find my ring?" She put it on the little finger of her left hand, and it went on as smoothly as if it had come home. "My ring!" she repeated, and looked at the prince with tears in her eyes. She sat on the grass under the low branches of the chestnuts, and turned the ring slowly around her finger with as much tenderness as if it had been a living thing.

"Why do you love your ring so much?" asked the prince, sitting down beside her.

She looked up at him. "My mother gave it to me on the day she died," she said. "I was only a little girl, but she told me, 'It will always help you in misfortune, and if you are ever in need, throw it into the sea. It will know how to find your saviour.'"

The prince smiled and took the girl's hands in his. "The ring did not give me a moment's peace until I found you here in the forest. I hope I may be your saviour. But tell me, what is your misfortune?"

The girl looked around anxiously, and whispered, "I live here with an old mountain troll, who makes me work like a slave." And she told him the sad tale of her life.

She had been born in a castle high among the mountains and would have become a fine and noble princess, but her mother had died when she was a child. When she was fifteen, a duke from another country captured the castle, murdered her father, and carried her away. She had lived in a tower of the foreign duke's palace and was given the best of everything: costly gowns, delicacies, and numerous servants to wait on her. But she was never allowed to leave the palace. Only from a window in her chamber could she see the outside world of flowering meadows, green woods, and the river that wound like a ribbon of silver through the valley. One day the duke came to her room and told her that in three months she would marry his son.

The girl looked at the prince with sad eyes. "It was the greatest misfortune and shame that could ever have befallen me. The duke's son was big and coarse as a giant, his face was red, and he was almost always drunk. I would rather have died than become his wife."

However, the girl had pretended that she would very much like to marry the duke's son. But first, she said, she wanted to make him a gift of a braided rope for the anchor of his sailing ship; when that was finished, she would happily become his bride. And so she began to braid a rope of the strongest hemp she could find, and soon it was so long it reached from her window all the way down to the valley.

✥ ❈ ✥

On the evening before the wedding, she locked herself in her little tower chamber, tied the rope to the window, and climbed down. She ran as fast as she could to hide in the forest, and there she crept into a dense thicket and fell into a deep sleep.

Next morning, she was awakened by a tickling on her forehead. When she opened her eyes she saw a terrifying face looking down at her. The troll of the mountain, who had been taking his morning walk through the forest, was poking her with a blade of grass. A long red tongue lolled from his mouth, and he had great furry black hands like a bear.

"I was so frightened," said the girl, "that I hardly dared breathe."

The troll had laughed horribly and said, "What luck to find you, little sweet one. I want someone to care for me, cook my food, carry my water and my wood, and be my companion." And so the troll caught her by the hair and carried her to his cave on the mountaintop. It was a deep, black cave, and even on the hottest summer day it was cold as a cellar and heavy drops of water trickled from the stones.

"Now I have served the mountain troll for three years," sighed the girl, "and every summer he tells me, 'Next Christmas, when you are a little fatter, I will eat you.'

"So I hardly dare eat, and I have not thought of anything but how to escape. One spring day I ran all the way down the mountainside to the river, hoping to cross to the other side. But there was no bridge, only the rapids and spray. So I took off my ring and threw it in the water and called out as my mother taught me:

> *Ring, ring, pulse and spring*
> *And my knight to me bring,*
> *A knight so good, a knight so brave,*
> *To rescue me, a helpless slave.*

"The ring disappeared into the water. But now," finished the girl, smiling, "the ring has found the knight who will help and save me." And she kissed the ring.

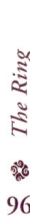

That moment they heard a strange, thundering sound.

"It is the troll of the mountain," the girl cried, and jumped up. "Quick! Quick! We must run as fast as we can."

They sped down the mountainside to where the prince's horse was grazing quietly by the river. Quickly the prince swung into the saddle, lifted the princess in front of him, and plunged into the water. Waves splashed over their heads, the horse panted and snorted and kicked in the river, and the mountain troll in the forest howled and bellowed like a pack of hungry wolves.

The prince and the girl rode for days and nights through forest and plain, across rivers and brooks, past groves and hedges. The horse never tired until they reached the prince's castle. There they arrived one moonlit night, and rode slowly along the seashore, the princess wrapped up in the prince's big cape.

She lifted a corner of the cape and looked down at the sand. "How strange," she said, with a smile on her face. "Looking at the shadow, it seems as if we were united, as one."

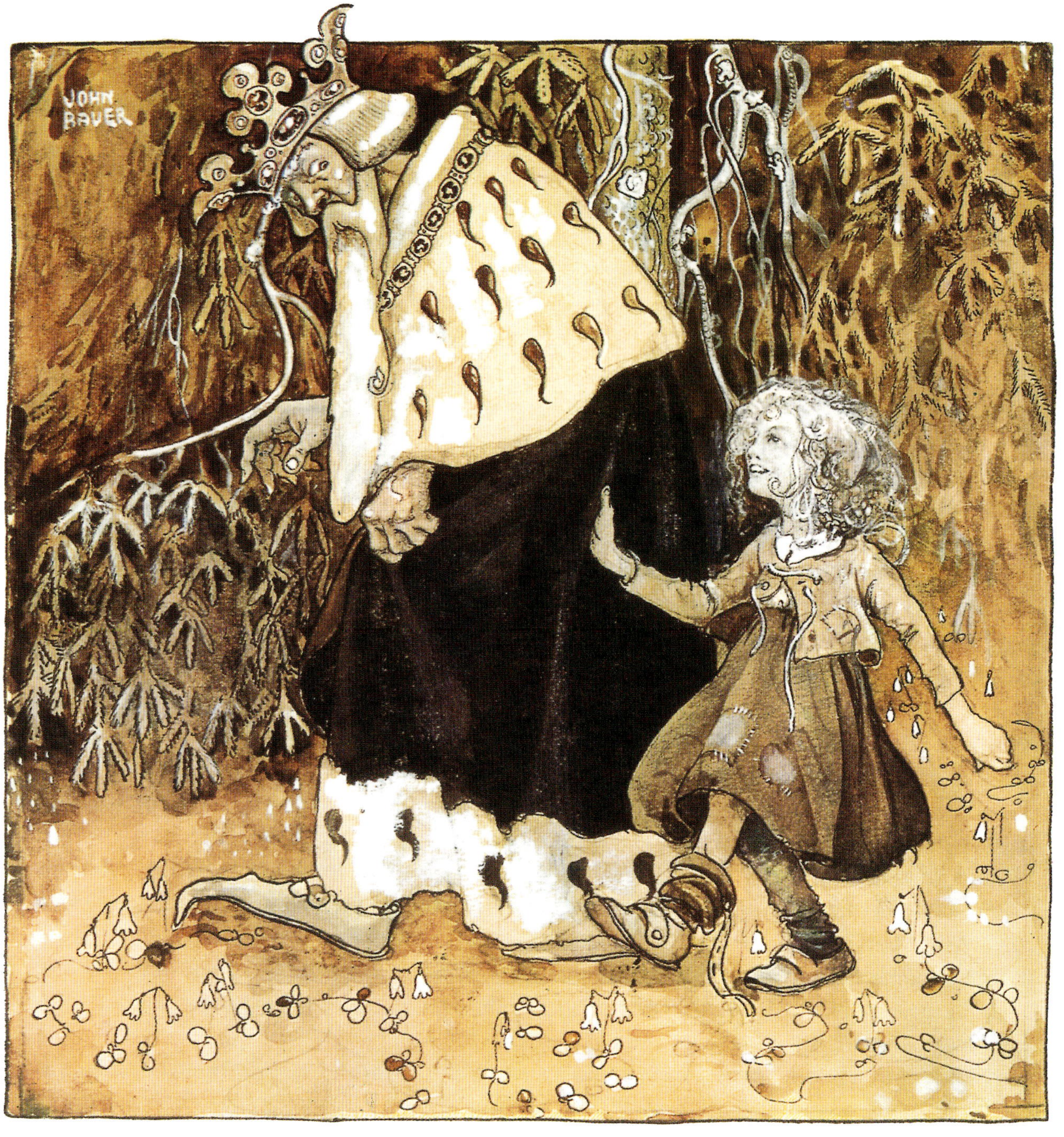
JOHN
BAUER

Linda-Gold and the Old King

Anna Wahlenberg

Long, long ago there lived an old king who was rather eccentric. People said he was odd because he had had many sorrows. His queen and children had died, and he himself said his heart had been torn apart. Who had done that and how it happened, he never told; but it was someone with claws, he said, and since then he imagined that everyone had claws on their hands.

No one was allowed to come nearer than two arms' lengths to the king. His valets were not allowed to touch him, and his dining-room steward had to place his food at the very edge of the table. The king had not shaken anyone's hand for many, many years. If people were careless enough not to remember about the two arms' lengths and came an inch closer, the king had them clapped in irons for a week to refresh their memory.

In all other ways, the old king was a good king. He governed his subjects well and justly. Everyone was devoted to him, and the only thing his people regretted was that he had not found a new queen, or chosen an heir to inherit the realm. When they asked him about this, however, he always said, "Show me someone who does not have claws and I will make that person my heir."

But no one ever appeared who, in the king's mind, did not have claws. The claws might be under the fingernails, or curled in the palm, but they were always there, he believed.

Now one day it happened that the old king was walking alone in the forest. He grew tired and sat down to rest on the moss and listen to the birds singing in the trees.

Suddenly a small girl rushed up the path, her hair streaming behind her. The king heard a growl behind him, and when he looked around, he saw in the trees a shaggy gray beast with flashing eyes and a grinning red mouth. It was a wolf, who wanted the little girl for breakfast. The old king rose and drew his sword, and straightaway the wolf turned in fear and ran back into the forest.

When the wolf had gone, the little girl began to weep and tremble. "You must walk home with me now," she said, "or else the wolf will chase me again."

"Must I?" asked the king, who was not accustomed to taking orders.

"Yes. And my mother will give you a loaf of white bread for your trouble. My name is Linda-Gold, and my father is the miller on the other side of the forest."

The king realized she was right. He couldn't very well let her be killed by the wolf, and so he decided to accompany her.

"You go first," he said. "I will follow behind you."

But the little girl did not dare walk first. "May I hold your hand?" she asked, and moved closer to him.

The king started, and looked closely at the little hand raised to his. "No, I am sure you have claws too, though you are so small," he said.

Linda-Gold's eyes filled with tears and she hid her hands behind her back. "My father says that I have claws too, but I have only forgotten to cut my nails." She looked ashamed and cast her eyes down at the ground. But then she asked if she might at least take hold of his mantle, and the king agreed to that. He simply could not make himself tell her to keep two arms' lengths away, for she was only a small child who would not understand.

So Linda-Gold skipped along beside the king and told him of her cottage and all her toys. She had so many beautiful things she wanted to show him: a cow made of pine cones, with matchsticks for legs; a boat made from an old wooden shoe, with burdock leaves for a sail; and, best of all, a doll her mother had sewn for her from an old brown apron and stuffed with yarn. It had a skirt made from the sleeve of a red sweater, and a blue ribbon at the neck, and her big brother had drawn a face on it with coal and put on a patch of leather for a nose.

The old king listened patiently to all her chattering, and smiled. He was sure her little hand had claws, yet he let it pull and jerk at his mantle as much as it wished.

But when Linda-Gold and the king came to the highway close to the mill, the king said goodbye. Now Linda-Gold could go the rest of the way home by herself.

But Linda-Gold did not want to say goodbye so soon. She clung to his arm and tugged it, and begged him to come with her. How could he not want white bread, which was so good? It couldn't be true that he did not want to look at her fine toys! She would let him play with her doll all the evening, if only he would come home with her. She would give him a present — the boat with the burdock-leaf sails — because he had saved her from the wolf.

When none of this helped, she at last asked the king where he lived.

"In the castle," he said.

"And what is your name?"

"Old Man Graybeard."

"Good. Then I will come to visit you, Old Man Graybeard." And she took off her little blue checked scarf and stood waving it as long as the king could see her — and he turned to look back quite often, because he thought her the sweetest little girl he had met in a long time.

Even after he had returned to the castle, he still thought of Linda-Gold, wondering if she really would come to visit him. He was worried because she did not want to keep her little hands at a respectful distance, but he could not deny that he longed to see her.

✢ ❦ ✢

The next morning, the king felt sure that Linda-Gold would not dare venture out so far for fear of the wolf, but then he clearly heard a child's voice calling from the palace yard. He went to the balcony and saw Linda-Gold with a rag doll under her arm. She was arguing with the gatekeeper. She said she must speak to Old Man Graybeard about something very important.

The gatekeeper just laughed at her and replied that no Old Man Graybeard lived there. Then Linda-Gold got angry. He mustn't say that, she insisted, for she herself knew very well Old Man Graybeard did live there. He had told her so himself.

Next, she went up to a lady-in-waiting who had just come outside and asked her advice. No, the lady-in-waiting had never heard of Old Man Graybeard either, and she too laughed heartily.

But Linda-Gold did not give up. She asked the cook, she asked the steward of the household, and she asked all the courtiers, who had begun to gather in the courtyard to stare at her. She turned red in the face as they all laughed, and her lower lip began to tremble. Her eyes were full of tears, but she still maintained firmly in a clear voice, "Old Man Graybeard must live here, because he told me so himself."

The king called from his balcony, "Yes, here I am, Linda-Gold."

Linda-Gold looked up, gave a shout of joy, and jumped up and down in excitement. "Do you see, do you see!" she called in triumph. "I told you he was here."

The courtiers could do nothing but stare in surprise. The king had to command twice that Linda-Gold be brought to him before anyone obeyed. It was no less a person than the royal court's Master of Ceremonies who led her to the king's chamber. When the door opened, Linda-Gold ran straight to the king and set her rag doll on his knee.

"I will give you this instead of the boat," she said, "because I thought that since you saved me from the wolf you should have the best thing of all."

The rag doll was the ugliest, most clumsy little bundle imaginable, but the old king smiled as if he were quite delighted with it.

"Isn't she sweet?" asked Linda-Gold.

"Yes, very."

"Kiss her, then."

And so the king kissed the doll.

"Since you like her, shouldn't you thank me?" demanded Linda-Gold.

"Thank you," said the king, nodding in a friendly way.

"That wasn't right," said Linda-Gold.

"Not right? How should it be then?"

"When you say thank you, you must also pat my cheek," said Linda-Gold.

And so the king had to pat her on the cheek; but it was a warm, soft little cheek, and not at all unpleasant to pat.

"And now—" said Linda-Gold.

"Is there something more?" asked the king.

"Yes! I would like to pat your cheek, too."

Here the king hesitated. This was really too much for him.

"Because, you see," Linda-Gold went on, "I cut my fingernails." She held up both her small, chubby hands for the king to see. He had to look at them whether he liked it or not.

And, truly, he could not see anything unusual on the pink fingertips. The nails were cut as close as a pair of scissors could, and there wasn't the trace of a claw.

"You can't say I have claws now, Graybeard," said Linda-Gold.

"No… Hmm… Well, pat my cheek, then."

Linda-Gold patted the old sunken cheeks, and soon a couple of tears came rolling down the old king's face. It was so long since he had known affection.

Now he took Linda-Gold in his arms and carried her to the balcony. "Here you see the one you have always longed for," he called to those in the courtyard.

A loud cry of joy broke out among them. "Hurrah for our little princess. Hurrah! Hurrah!" they shouted.

Surprised and bewildered, Linda-Gold turned to the king and asked him what they meant.

"It means they like you because you have fine small hands that have no claws and never scratch," he said.

Then he kissed the two little hands so that everyone could see, and from below the people shouted again, "Hurrah for our little princess!"

And that is how Linda-Gold became a princess and, when the time came, inherited the kingdom of the old king.

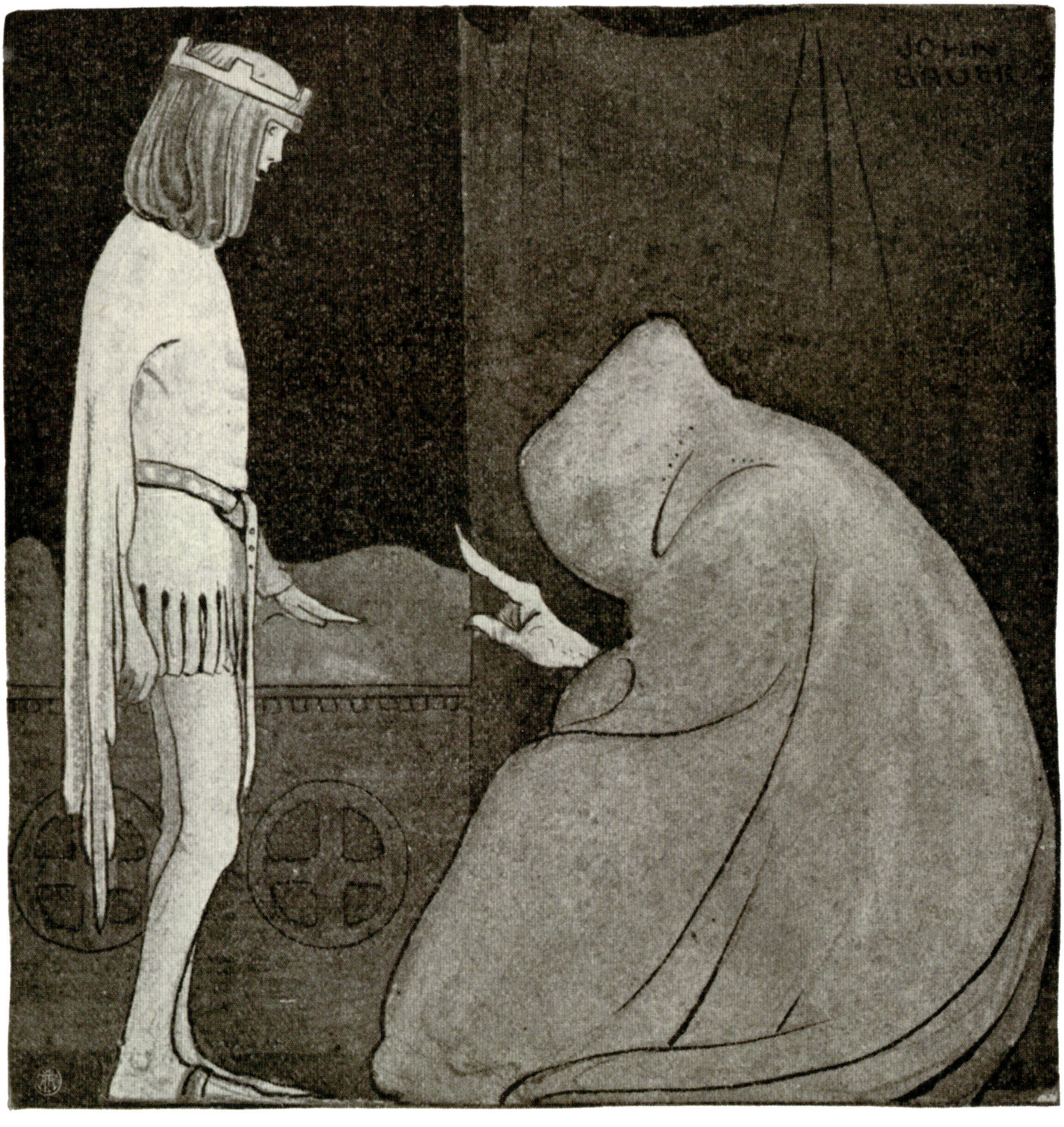
JOHN
BAUER

The Prince Without a Shadow

Jeanna Oterdahl

Once upon a time, there was a handsome young prince who was the joy and pride of the whole kingdom. When the prince crossed the marketplace, crowds followed to greet him. Little girls threw flowers, boys cheered, and the prince greeted everyone with his soft smile, which would melt the coldest heart. No one was as joyful or as clever or as kind-hearted as the young prince. If he saw need and suffering, he always tried to help. So it was that peace and prosperity ruled in the whole kingdom.

However, the king and the queen had another child, a little princess of five years, who was unwell and pale. Usually she sat in her high armchair by the window playing with flowers that her brother had picked for her in the palace gardens. Every now and then she would smile wanly at the children outside. Sometimes the prince would take her out in a richly decorated carriage pulled by two fine horses, but the princess took no joy in this. She was too sick and tired, and everyone was heartbroken to see her so.

It was most difficult for the king and queen, who dearly loved their healthy, happy son but could not help loving their unwell, sad daughter all the more. The doctors of the kingdom had prescribed drops and ointments from all over the world, but in vain. The princess became paler and weaker, and soon it looked as if she would die. The queen stayed with her day and night, the king in his sorrow forgot to rule over his realm, and the young prince racked his brains to think of some way of helping his little sister.

One night the prince and the queen were at her bedside. At the door sat a page, but, though he kept his hand on his dagger, he had fallen asleep. Even the two chamberlains had fallen asleep in front of the fire. It was quite still in the room; only the breathing of the sleepers could be heard. The queen, who had not slept a wink the night before, finally slumped back in her chair and nodded off. Only the prince was awake — wide awake — and watched the moonlight shining onto his sister's face, filling it with light.

After the prince had sat for a long time without moving, he went to the window to stretch his legs. The stars in the sky showed him that it was midnight, and just then the watch in the tower blew the horn to mark the hour. When the prince turned, he saw a strange figure sitting in a gray coat with the cape pulled low over its face.

That must be Death, the prince thought fearfully, afraid that he had come to take his little sister.

The figure looked up with a strange expression on its face, and said, "I am not Death. See, I have neither scythe nor hourglass. I am the man who gathers shadows. If you will give me your shadow, your sister's illness will vanish and she will become the most beautiful princess."

"My shadow?" asked the prince, and he saw how the moonlight made it long and black on the floor. "Why do you want my shadow?"

"That is my business," the stranger answered. "Either you give me your shadow and your sister regains her health, or you keep it and she remains ill. Incidentally, Death *is* close by — I just saw him at the city gates."

The prince looked at his pale sister, and then at his own shadow. As far as he could remember, he had never had any use for his shadow. Why shouldn't he be able to survive without it? And what a joy it would be to have a strong and healthy sister, and to see his parents happy again. All the people would say, "There goes our noble prince who saved his sister by giving away his shadow."

"No, no!" said the stranger. "If you agree to the exchange, you must swear never to tell a soul what we have agreed tonight. And if you break your promise, your sister will in an instant fall dead."

"You seem to be able to read my thoughts," said the prince. "I feel uneasy about that. However, I agree to the exchange. Take my shadow and make my sister better. I promise not to say a word to anyone."

"Then we are agreed," said the stranger, and rose from the chair. He was as thin as a shadow himself. He bent over, picked up the prince's shadow and put it in his bag, and disappeared.

The prince looked around the room in surprise. Nothing had changed. Everyone was asleep, and the sand ran through the hourglass as before. Only one thing was different — no matter which way the prince turned, he could not see the smallest trace of a shadow.

"Ah well!" said the prince to himself. "What use is the shadow to me?"

He leaned over the bed to look at his sister, and leapt with surprise. Her pale cheeks had some red color, her fine lips were now rosy and smiling. The girl was breathing steadily and seemed healthy, as if resting after a long day of play. The prince was so happy he forgot all worries about his shadow. He sank into his chair and cried for joy.

☩ ✣ ☩

Next morning, when news of the princess's wondrous recovery spread, there was great joy in the palace, the city, and the whole kingdom. The king and queen could hardly believe their eyes when they saw her running around in the palace gardens. When the prince took her for a ride in the carriage, she asked to take the reins herself, and called "Gee up!" to the horses, so loudly it could be heard afar. Children waved at her while she stood on the coach-box, throwing them raisins and spiced cakes.

Everyone was so astounded that they did not notice the prince's missing shadow. He barely had time to think of it himself. However, after a while, he did observe a kind of absence or emptiness, particularly in the evenings, when other people's shadows grew into long giants. It was unpleasant to have the sun at his back, and he tried as often as possible to face the sun, so as not to be reminded that he was now different from other humans.

But people began to notice at last. The ladies of the court whispered in corners, and the courtiers looked at him strangely.

One evening as he was riding his white horse, children surrounded him joyfully as usual. He was feeling light-hearted, for he had briefly forgotten what was troubling him. But as he bent down to lift one of the children into his saddle, a shrill little voice exclaimed, "Look, look, the horse has a shadow, but the prince doesn't."

And then a hundred little voices were calling, "The horse has a shadow, but the prince doesn't!"

Now it's over, thought the prince, and he spurred his horse on to ride back to the palace.

The next day the whole city talked of how the prince had lost his shadow through wizardry. It was as if they had completely forgotten that he was their beloved prince. Now they stuck their heads together to discuss what unimaginable treasures the prince must have gained by selling his shadow, for it was clear that he must have profited from it somehow. At every street corner they spoke of it, and it did not take long before children were pointing at the prince, and even throwing stones and cursing him, when he went out on one of his ever more seldom walks. All this made the prince so heavy-hearted that the little princess cried at the change in her merry brother.

When the prince saw that even his father and mother were affected by the suspicions of the town, he decided to leave his home and kingdom for ever.

"Dear mother and dear father," he said. "I see that you too are dissatisfied with me. So I will no longer trouble you with my presence. Give the kingdom to my sister instead. Accept my thanks and farewell!"

The king and queen's hearts softened at that, and the queen began to weep.

"Just tell me, my dear son, what have you done with your shadow?" she asked.

"My shadow has gone," answered the prince, and lowered his head.

The king became angry. "We can all see that!" he shouted. "What we want to know is where it is!"

"I don't know," said the prince. "I only know it's gone."

"You are the most obstinate, ungrateful boy who ever lived!" the king exclaimed, rising from his throne. "Leave my kingdom and never return!"

The poor prince bowed again before his parents, kissed his little sister in parting and cut one of her locks as a keepsake. Then he left.

He wandered far and wide, until he no longer heard his own language spoken, and then he wandered through another three kingdoms. In the fourth kingdom he came to a wild oak forest.

"Here I will stay," he said to himself, "here in this forest among the wild animals. Perhaps they will be more charitable than people."

The prince's parents soon regretted their hardness.

"He may have lost his shadow, but what of it?" the king mused. "It is even quite proper that the prince is different from the crowd. Perhaps it was the special blessing of a powerful fairy? I shall send out messengers to find him."

"Yes," sighed the queen. "Fetch our son back or I may never be happy again."

Five hundred riders were sent forth through the whole kingdom and the neighboring realms to find the prince and fetch him back. But day after day passed, month after month. After a year, most of the riders had returned without having found a trace of him.

After three years, the last rider returned. He said that more than a hundred leagues from the kingdom he had found a child who said it had seen a youth without a shadow. But the child had no idea what became of him. That was the best the riders could do for the king and queen.

Over the years the little princess now grew into a beautiful girl — but she was not really happy. She could not forget her brother, who had always been happy and kind to her, and she kept wondering how she could find him again. One day she sat at the feet of her parents, as she liked to do.

"Last night I had such a strange dream," she said. "I was a little girl again, and ill, and my dear brother was watching by me. My mother and all the servants had gone to sleep; only he was awake. Suddenly a man in a gray coat appeared and made a bargain with my brother. He would make me better if my brother would give his shadow."

The king and queen paled. "Now I remember," said the queen. "It was during the night you recovered. The servants had nodded off one after another, and finally I fell asleep too. It was around this time that we noticed your brother's shadow had disappeared. The truth must be showing itself in your dream."

Thereupon the king made the dream known in every church of the land, and it did not take long to restore the people's love and worship for their prince. At every street corner, people stood and discussed what they could do to find him again. The princess, however, went to the king and asked, "Father, let me go and look for my brother who left because of me."

When the king saw her determination, he had to agree to let her go. He wanted to give her a great company of followers, but she asked to go alone. She dressed as a simple shepherdess and only kept the pearl necklace she had worn as a child. She thought her brother might recognize her by it. Then she bade farewell and went on her way.

Mile after mile she walked, and soon she was out of the kingdom. She asked everyone she met if they had seen the prince without a shadow, but no one had heard of him. Most thought she was mad and gave her some milk or a piece of bread and let her sleep in the hay. But the princess did not give up hope.

It was late one evening when she knocked on the door of a hut in a forest. On entering, she saw a red-eyed old woman who was so wrinkled she must be a hundred years old. "Good evening, dear Mother," the princess greeted her. "As you are so old, you will be wise. Tell me, have you ever heard of the prince without a shadow?"

The old one looked at the princess and nodded. "So you are his sister. I knew you would come, but it took a long time."

When the princess heard that the old one knew who she was, she felt so happy that she threw her arms around her and said, "Please, show me the way to my brother!"

But the old woman told her things could not be rushed. Only his own shadow would know the way to the prince, and the shadow was with the man in a gray coat who lived at the end of the world.

So the princess asked the woman to show her the way to the end of the world.

"What will you give me if I show you the way?" asked the old one.

"Anything you want," replied the girl.

"Give me your beauty," said the old one. And as the princess agreed, she passed her hand three times over the face of the girl, and in an instant the beauty had passed from one to the other. The princess's eyes were small and ugly, her cheeks were gray, her mouth as wide as a toad's, and her golden locks turned into matted straggles. The princess sighed when the old woman handed her a looking-glass, but then she laughed again.

"It's lucky I have the pearl necklace," she said, "or my brother would not believe me to be his sister."

The old woman went to get a ball of wool from a chest and told her, "Throw it in front of you when you leave tomorrow morning. It will bring you to the end of the world."

The princess thanked her, and next morning, after she had rested, she threw the ball of wool. It rolled in front of her no faster than she could walk, and when she wanted to rest, she caught the ball easily and put it in her pocket. She continued her journey day after day, and how long she went on like this she did not know.

One day as she was going through a dark forest, a troll suddenly jumped in her path, picked up the ball of wool and swung it over his head, laughing loudly.

"Good day, Mr Troll," she said, her voice quavering. "Please give me my ball of wool back. Without it I cannot find my brother." She knelt before the troll, weeping bitterly.

"What will you give me for it?" asked the troll.

"Whatever you want," she answered.

"Give me your youth!" said the troll. Then he passed his hand three times over her head and the princess felt a coldness pass through her. Her limbs became stiff and her skin wrinkled.

The troll gave her the ball of wool, but when she rolled it she found she could only follow it half as fast as before. "Dear little ball of wool," she called, "please roll a bit slower, I'm an old woman now."

The ball listened and immediately rolled so slowly that the princess could follow it. She had to rest more often, and often she asked herself whether this road would ever come to an end.

Finally she came to a great blue shimmering sea. Far out on a peninsula stood a castle, and the ball of wool came to rest in front of the gates. The princess knew this was the castle at the end of the world, and the home of the man with the gray coat. She lifted her old, stiff hand and knocked on the gate. The man in the gray coat opened the door himself.

"At last you are here," he said, "just as I expected. But you don't think I'll give you your brother's shadow without getting something in return?"

"No," answered the princess. "I have learned on my way here that one does not receive anything without giving something in return. I know that you want from me what you gave my brother that night in return for his shadow. So take my health and let the shadow of my brother show me the way to him."

The gray man laid his hands on her head and the princess felt the illness taking hold of her. At the same time, the shadow of her brother appeared on the ground beside her. It was the shadow of a slim youth, just as she remembered him. Silently and slowly the shadow moved over the ground and the sick, old woman followed it with unsteady steps.

I hope I can survive until I find my brother, she thought.

After they had traveled a long time, they came to a clear spring. The princess was thirsty and she bent achingly over to drink. When she saw her old, feeble face, she said to the shadow, "I will not tell my brother who I am. It would make him too sad to see me like this. Good shadow, promise me you won't betray me!"

The shadow appeared to nod, and she was satisfied.

After countless miles, they came to a deep forest. The shadow glided silently over the grass and the princess followed, though every step brought her pain and she could hardly move for tiredness. Finally the shadow stopped at a low hut made of woven branches. A young man with a sad face sat in the doorway and fed the wild animals gathered around him. The shadow glided behind him, and the princess recognized her brother. She stood before him and spoke his name.

"Who are you, that you know my name?" he asked.

"Call me your unknown friend," she replied. "I bring greetings from your home and from the whole kingdom. You are welcome to all, and they long to see you again, and for you to forgive them."

"I have been driven from my country, for I had no shadow. And because I shall never get it back, I will never return," the prince said solemnly.

"Your shadow guided me here," said the princess. "Turn around and look!"

She told him how the king and queen missed their son and regretted their harshness, and how they had tried to find him for many years. Yet she said nothing about the princess and evaded all questions the prince asked about her. At last she persuaded the prince to return next morning to his kingdom with his shadow, in the company of the old woman.

Overnight he let her rest in the hut on a bed of soft moss and leaves, and next morning he called to a stag to carry her so that she would not have to walk any more. As he lifted her on to the stag's back, he recognized the pearl necklace and said, "That is my sister's necklace. How do you come to have it? Tell me of her as we walk."

The princess thought he would never leave her in peace until she answered his questions. So she said, "Your sister has been dead for a long time."

When the prince heard this, he put his hands to his face and wept. "Now I understand why my shadow has returned to me," he said. "But I would rather have lived the rest of my life without it, if I knew that my sister was alive and happy."

Hardly had the prince spoken these words than she felt her health returning, and she understood that the power of the gray man had been broken.

After a time they came to a dark forest, and the princess recognized it as the place where she had met the troll. She saw it in a thicket, beckoning to her, as if he wanted something.

"Let me get off here for a while," she told the prince. "I have an old acquaintance here in the forest whom I must visit."

The prince helped her down and sat down to wait. But when she came back, he hardly recognized her. She walked quickly and easily and swung herself onto the stag without help. Then she smiled at him, and although she was still ugly, she was strangely younger. He opened his mouth to ask questions, but she stopped him, saying, "My acquaintance had to pay me my due."

They continued their journey, and after a time came to the tumbledown hut where the hundred-year-old woman lived. The princess jumped from the back of the stag and went into the hut to return the gray woollen ball that had helped her so much.

When she came out of the hut, the prince could not believe his eyes. Instead of an ugly girl with straggly hair and a wide toad's mouth, there was a beautiful maiden before him. Only her old clothes, shoes and the pearl necklace reminded him of his companion.

The princess went to him, took his hands and said, "My dear brother, now the last of my debts has been repaid. Do you recognize your sister?"

The prince, who had slowly begun to understand, took his sister into his arms and cried for joy.

"How could I ever have been happy at home without my little sister at my side?" he asked, and he played with the pearls in her necklace as he used to do. "Now we shall always be together!"

And he showed her the lock of hair that he had kept when he wandered out into the world.

At last they came to their kingdom and home. There was great rejoicing, and no one was in the slightest bit worried any more about whether or not the prince had a shadow.

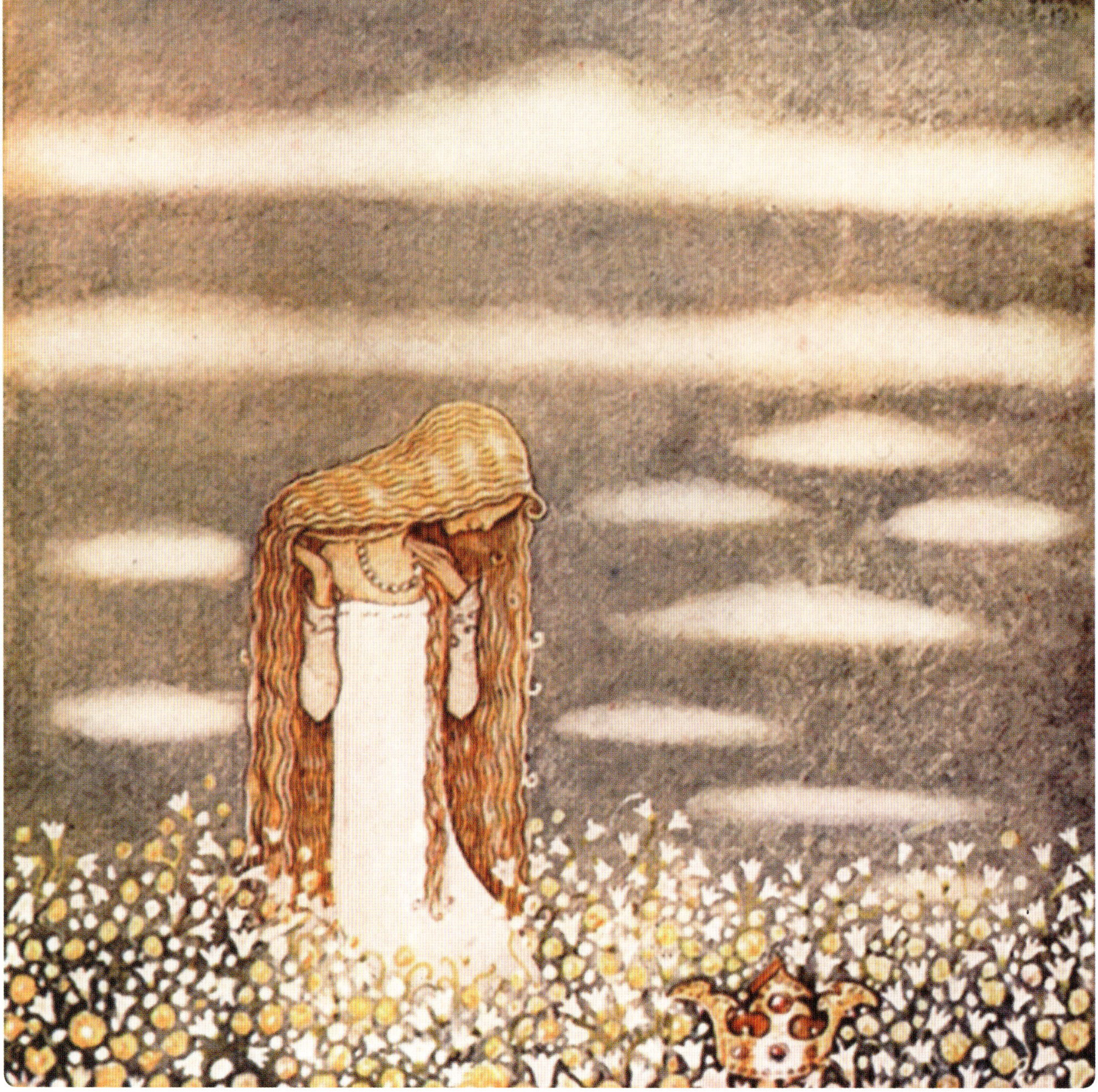

The Queen

Anna Wahlenberg

Many hundreds of years ago, there lived a maiden who was famous in several kingdoms. Adelgunda was indeed a remarkable young woman. She was delicate and pale as a lily, but it was not her beauty that people spoke of. Nor was it her good sense, though one and all could see intelligence shining on her brow.

No, what Adelgunda was renowned for were her two wonderful eyes, which could speak much more plainly than her lips. Her eyes could also see better than anyone else's; they saw what people were thinking and things that lay hidden deep in their souls.

Yet no one was afraid of Adelgunda's eyes, which rested long on good and beautiful things. When her eyes saw something ugly and evil, they said so, yet with sorrow and compassion, not hatred and contempt. Adelgunda's eyes spoke a language that everyone understood.

Anyone who met the young woman became fond of her and left hoping to see her again. Only the really wicked and those with uneasy consciences shunned her. They never dared show themselves in the neighborhood of the old castle where she lived with her father, Sir Hubert.

But one day a messenger announced the arrival of a very special guest. Prince Sigmund, who would one day inherit the realm from his father, the king, was wooing a beautiful princess in a powerful nearby kingdom. The prince was now on his way to meet the princess, to see if they really suited each other. And since his road took him past Sir Hubert's castle, Sigmund decided to visit and meet Adelgunda, of whom he had heard so many remarkable things.

Adelgunda was also curious about the prince, for she had heard how brave, handsome, and chivalrous he was, and how much his people loved him. But suppose she saw something in him that others did not see, something which was not beautiful? Her eyes would speak of it, since they could not hide anything they saw. How terrible that would be! And how ashamed her father would be if such a thing happened to the young prince in his home.

At last Adelgunda decided what to do. She would hide and steal a glance at the prince before he entered the castle. If she saw anything that her eyes ought not to reveal, she would run into the forest and not return until Prince Sigmund had left.

Silently, she slipped from the castle and walked towards the road. When she saw a cloud of dust at the top of the hill, she hid behind a wild rose bush, where she could watch without being seen.

After a while, a cloud of dust rose at the top of the hill and four riders approached at a fast gallop. One looked more distinguished than the others, and Adelgunda realized it must be the prince. Just as the riders reached the rose bush where she was hiding, the prince's horse stumbled on a stone and fell heavily.

His frightened companions reined in, dismounted, and gathered anxiously around Prince Sigmund to see if he had been hurt. But he was already on his feet examining his horse, which was trying to stand.

"I am unharmed," he said, "but my horse has sprained a leg."

"Will Your Highness take my horse then?" asked the nearest knight, bringing up his mount.

But the prince slapped him warmly on the shoulder. "Should one of my trusted and faithful comrades walk while I ride?" he asked. "No, that will never do. Let's ask at that farm cottage if they will lend us a horse."

The knight rode towards a nearby cottage, and soon he returned with a large, heavy dray horse, shaggy and unkempt, as such horses sometimes are. He dismounted, took the saddle from the lame horse and strapped it on the borrowed one, and was just about to swing himself onto its back, leaving his own horse for the prince when again the prince rebuffed him with a warm smile.

"I am the one who fell," he said. "I shall ride old Ned." With that, he threw himself onto the saddle, caught the reins of his limping horse, and rode on at the head of his companions.

As Adelgunda watched Prince Sigmund riding so tall on the strong but homely dray horse, he seemed as handsome as a dream. She knew that from then on she would think about him every hour of every day of her life.

☩ ❈ ☩

She walked home in a dream, and she was still dreaming when she went to her room, braided pearls in her hair and put on a white gown with silver embroidery.

Only when a lady-in-waiting knocked on the door with a message from her father to hurry to meet their distinguished guest did she come to her senses. She started in fright, for she suddenly realized that she could not meet the prince. Her eyes would tell him, plainly and clearly, that to her he was the finest man on earth. A noble maiden must never make such a confession to a man, much less to a prince who was so far above her in birth and rank.

Yet Adelgunda said, "Tell my father I am coming," for it was too late to run and hide in the forest.

Instead, she ran to her mother's old room, opened a cupboard, and picked out the thickest white veil she could find. Quickly, she threw the veil over her head and walked into the hall where they were waiting for her.

A murmur of surprise rose from everyone in the room as she stepped over the threshold. After she had greeted their honored guest, her father asked, "Why are you wearing a veil, Adelgunda?"

"Forgive me, Father, but I am not used to the company of princes," she answered.

Sir Hubert smiled and turned to Prince Sigmund. "I am sure she will soon become less shy," he said.

They sat down at the table, with the prince between the knight and his daughter. The prince had eyes for no one but Adelgunda. She seemed to him graceful and gentle; her voice was musical and her words were wise. When she lifted her veil a little to put a wine goblet to her lips, he caught a glimpse of her face, which made him yearn to see it unveiled.

After the meal, they rose from the table, but Adelgunda slipped behind the other guests in the hope of being able to leave the room unnoticed, and then run from the castle. However, she soon found the prince standing before her.

"I have heard about your eloquent eyes, noble maid," he said. "Won't you let me have the pleasure of seeing them, as others do?"

She bowed her head low. "I cannot," she whispered.

"Then I must believe you have seen something in me that you do not wish your eyes to speak of."

"Oh, no. No," she exclaimed in a troubled voice.

"Then please lift your veil."

But Adelgunda stayed still, wishing she could die.

Her father joined them and looked at Adelgunda with puzzled brows. "What sort of childishness is this?" he asked. "Take off your veil at once."

"I cannot," Adelgunda replied, in a voice so low it could hardly be heard.

Sir Hubert was about to tear the veil from his daughter's head when the prince stopped him and bade the company a stiff farewell. He did not wish to force Adelgunda to obey him.

He and his retinue rode quickly from the castle, and Adelgunda remained standing in the hall, weeping bitterly and without a reply to all her father's reproaches.

Word spread quickly throughout the realm that Adelgunda had not let the prince look into her eyes. People asked each other what she could have seen in him that she could not speak of. So strong was their faith in her gift of reading people's minds that they whispered that she must have discovered something wicked in the prince, although he had always been thought of as good and righteous.

The whispers spread farther and farther, until at last they reached the court of the powerful king whose daughter Sigmund was wooing. When the princess heard the whispers, she refused to discuss marriage any more, and asked him to leave at once. She said Sigmund might return only once Adelgunda had lifted her veil and shown that her eyes had nothing evil to say of him.

The prince went back to his own kingdom angered by this insult, and yet even at home he saw only mistrust and suspicion in people's eyes. His anger turned to sorrow, and he locked himself in his rooms, cursing the day he had met Adelgunda.

There was one person, however, who was even more grieved than the prince by all that had happened, and that was Adelgunda herself. When she heard how he had suffered for her sake, all she could think was that she must do everything in her power to absolve him from blame.

She asked her father to go to the court and request that the king call together all the knights and ladies of the realm on a certain day — as many people as possible from far and near. There, Adelgunda would say something about the prince that would dispel all suspicions.

Sir Hubert set out at once to deliver his daughter's message, which was received with pleasure by both the king and the prince. Adelgunda, they believed, would soon appear without her veil, and then everyone would see that her eyes had nothing evil to tell.

☩ ✢ ☩

From every corner of the kingdom, knights and liegemen were summoned, and their wives and daughters came too. On the appointed day, half the throne room was filled with nobility, and the burghers and peasants so crowded the other half that no one could move an elbow.

When all the guests were assembled, a door was opened, and Adelgunda and her father entered. But the prince and the king saw that Adelgunda was still wearing her veil. Their faces became troubled and their guests were offended.

As Adelgunda reached the throne, she curtsied deeply to the king, and even more deeply to Prince Sigmund. Indeed, she made such a long, low curtsy that the prince sprang up and offered her his hand.

She turned to the king, and then to the whole gathering. "I have heard that some people are suspicious of Prince Sigmund because I did not wish to lift my veil before him. I have come here today to tell you what my eyes have seen. They have seen that there is no more chivalrous, noble and good man than he on the whole wide earth."

"Then lift your veil and let us see that your lips do not tell us one thing and your eyes another," said the king.

"That I cannot do," she answered.

"Then no one will believe you," said the old king, his eyes ablaze.

"No one will believe you," everyone called out angrily.

Adelgunda stood where she was, with her head still bowed. Then she took one step towards Prince Sigmund, and slowly lifted the veil from her pale, beautiful face.

The eyes that rested on the prince shone like two wonderful stars and told him, plainly and clearly, what a young maiden must never say to any man, much less to a prince. And it was not only the prince who saw what they said; everyone present saw, too. Now they knew why she had not wanted to lift her veil, and suddenly the throne room was so still you could have heard a handkerchief flutter to the floor.

"May I go now?" asked Adelgunda. "Come, Father."

She took Sir Hubert's hand, and they walked slowly through the throng of people.

But before they had reached the door, a voice rang out over the heads of the guests. "Close the doors."

It was the prince speaking, and the guards hastened to obey him. Then the prince threw himself on his knees before the king.

"Sir," he pleaded. "Will we let the queen depart?"

"The queen?" asked the king.

"Yes, the queen. For is she not a queen among women? To me at least, there will never be anyone else."

The king looked at the upturned faces before him. "Do all of you, too, say that she is a queen?" he asked.

A roar of "Yes" rose from every corner of the room, from nobles and peasants, from young and old. It echoed and rang until the old castle walls reverberated.

"Since you all say so, so be it," said the old king. "We will not let the queen depart."

He rose, stepped from his throne, and walked the length of the room until he stood in front of the noble maiden. Then he took her by the hand and led her slowly back through the joyous crowd. Before the throne, he placed her hand in the young prince's. Then everyone saw that Prince Sigmund's eyes too could speak. Adelgunda saw in his eyes the same message that he had seen in her own.

The two stood in silence, hand in hand, while cheers rose around them, so strong and loud it seemed they would never stop.

About the Authors

Cyrus Granér (1870–1937) was a writer and a composer. From 1907 to 1915 he edited *Bland tomtar och troll* (*Among Gnomes and Trolls*), an annual Christmas book of fairy tales that helped make John Bauer popular.

Helena Nyblom (1843–1926) was born in Copenhagen. She had her first short story published in 1875 and went on to be published widely. In 1905 she won the Iduns book prize with her novel *Högvalla* and in 1923 she was awarded the Swedish Medal for Art and Literature.

Harald Östenson was a widely published author whose stories appeared in the well-known children's magazine *Folkskolans barntidning* (*Elementary Schoolchild's Magazine*). He was also the editor of *Till föräldrar* (*For Parents*), a parenting magazine founded in 1897.

Jeanna Oterdahl (1879–1965) was a teacher, author, lecturer and poet in Gothenburg. Her children's books include the *Blommornas bok* (*The Flower Book*, 1905, with illustrations by Elsa Beskow).

Alfred Smedberg (1850–1925) was a teacher and author known for his fairy tales, poems and humorous writing.

Anna Wahlenberg (1858–1933) was born in Stockholm. A poet and author, Wahlenberg wrote many fairy and folk tales. John Bauer's first commission as a student was to illustrate her collection *Länge, länge sedan* (*Long, Long Ago*).

Acknowledgments

The following stories are reprinted by kind permission of the respective literary executors: *'The Four Big Trolls and Little Peter Pastureman'* by Cyrus Granér; *'The Prince Without a Shadow'* by Jeanna Oterdahl.

With thanks to the following for permission to use the images on the pages indicated: Bonnier Carlsen Bokförlag, Stockholm: 62, 68, 104, 111, 112, 114, 116; Göteborgs Konstmuseum, Gothenburg: 41 (photograph: Ebbe Carlsson), 47 (photograph: Sixten Sandell); Jönköpings Läns Museum, Jönköping: 74, 78 (photographs by Göran Sandstedt); National Museum, Stockholm: 80 (photograph: Åsa Lundén); private ownership, most photographs Jönköpings Läns Museum, Jönköping: 18, 23, 25, 31, 34, 36, 54, 71, 86, 92, 96.

Photos taken from Wikimedia Commons: p. 8 John and Putte by Esther Bauer; John Bauer at work by Calla Sundbeck; A young John Bauer by Atalier Lindhéborgs, Jönköping.

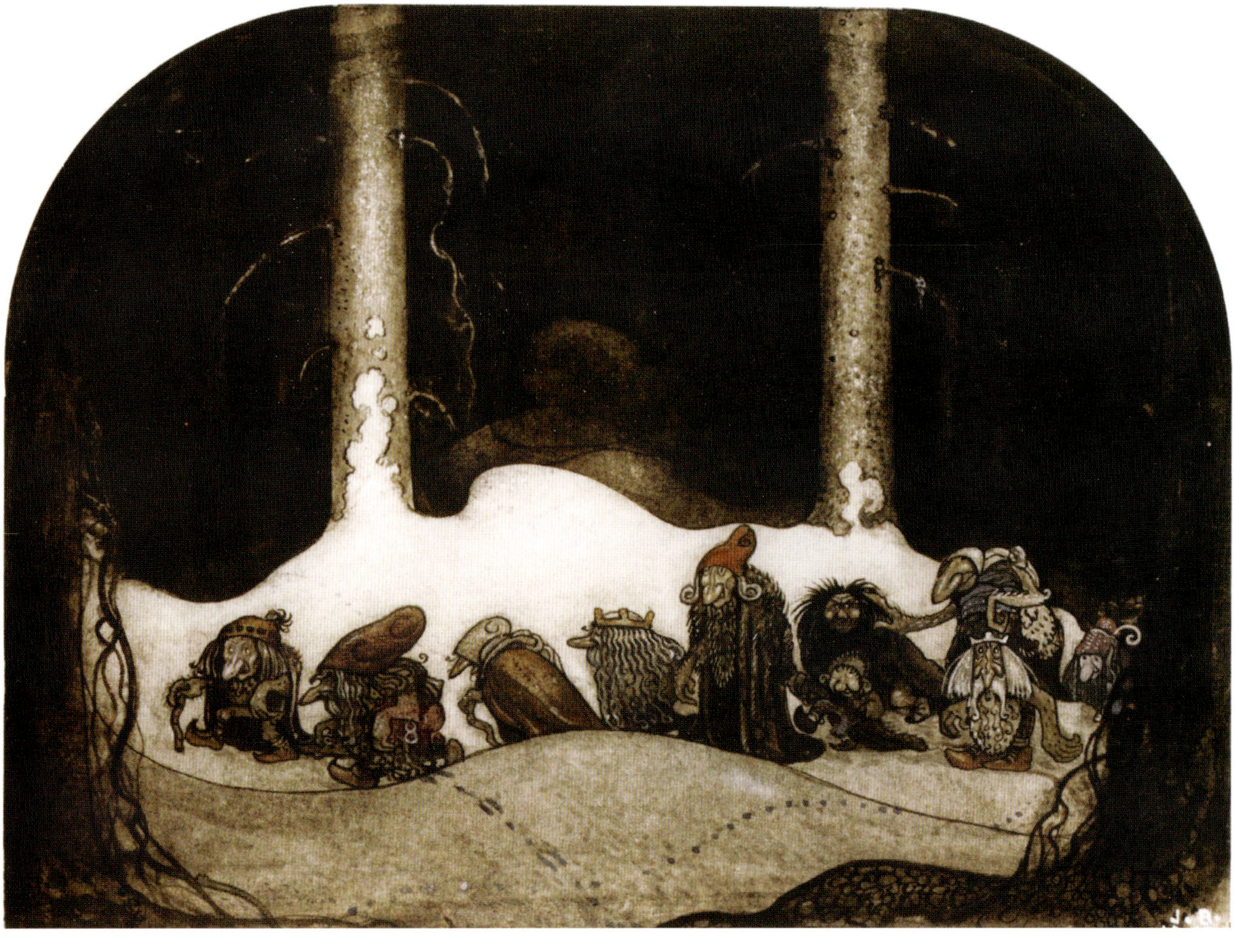